THE STAINED PASHMINA

Bijoy Munshi

Vitasta

To Dad,
Long before I saw the light,
you confronted life with all your might.
Hard, as it seems,
you departed on a beautiful flight.
Today, as I look at the stars,
shining through the night,
I try to feel what would have been,
had you lived to continue this fight.

Published by
Renu Kaul Verma
Vitasta Publishing Pvt Ltd
4348/4C, Ansari Road, Daryaganj
New Delhi - 110 002
info@vitastapublishing.com

ISBN: 978-81-19670-85-7

First Edition 2024
MRP ₹350

This novel is entirely a work of fiction. Names, characters, events and incidents are entirely imaginary. Reference to real places, actual regions, institutions or community practices has been made in a fictitious manner. Any resemblance to actual persons, living or dead or actual events is purely coincidental.

Edited by Vichitra Goel
Typeset & Cover Design by Somesh Kumar Mishra
Printed at Chaman Enterprises, New Delhi

Contents

My Birthday

Delhi 2019

In July 2019, on my 29th birthday, I received a write-up with birthday greetings in a PDF on WhatsApp. The number was unknown. I tried to search for the number online, and it showed a name–Yoginder Sharma, Solan. I failed to understand if the content was a piece of imagination or a pivotal truth hidden from me since birth. I wanted to pick up the phone, dial my mother and ask her to verify everything. At the end of the greetings was a message: 'Hope you recognise this handwriting and want to find out more. Follow the lead.'

Ten years ago, we had received two couriers at our ancestral home, and my mother had asked me not to pay attention to them. They comprised torn pages from a diary in the same handwriting but were about poetry and family. This one was completely different. I started looking for old pictures on my laptop. I wanted to match the handwriting and make sure it was the same.

The write-up was about the man from whom I had inherited my passion for writing. The man who was snatched from us in a road accident when I was just a year old. It was a cruel game of fate that left my mother hanging onto life by a thread.

Riyaz Dar, my father, was a civil engineer working with a private organisation based in New Delhi. For an avid traveller like him, wandering in the mountains was like oxygen. Almost all the stories that my mother told about him were based on the beauty of the mountains they explored together in their two years of togetherness. His kindness, intellect, simple mannerisms and contentment with life were the major points I heard of as a kid. I was often told that he excelled at his work and was extremely persuasive.

I recollected the story about the terror attack in which my grandfather had lost his life, but I wasn't told about my father killing anyone.

'Why have I received this write-up?' I pondered. 'Was this a fictional piece of writing that he dreamed of publishing, or was this the dangerous path of truth they never let me tread on?' There were questions in my mind, with no one to answer them.

I tried to search for the sender on social networking sites, but he seemed like a ghost. There were no social footprints. The mountains were calling me to unravel the truth.

Before I could overthink, I booked an evening bus to

Solan for the next day. There was no way I could leave this trail unexplored. I knew there would be many dead ends, but I was determined. It took me the whole night and the next morning to get a few contacts to help me in the hill town. Having influential relatives was always a major advantage, but now, I wanted to be as discreet as possible. A few friends helped me with the numbers and addresses of a few individuals in the administration. I thought only people in authority could help, but realised later that help comes from unknown quarters when you are in need.

Blood-Stained Snow

1987

Hints of snow covered the courtyard outside my house. The inhabitants of our peaceful hamlet were fast asleep. Shops were closed, and lanes deserted. A strong breeze made its presence felt, hitting the wooden walls of our house. I was on the stairs, looking through the window. My mind meandered towards the conversation I overheard at the grocery store that evening. I headed towards my room to continue writing my dream novel when my father called out my name.

'Riyaz, let's have some tea. Come down.' It distracted me. I ignored him for a second as my mind was engrossed in a fantasy world. He called out again, and I came out of my musings. I rushed downstairs and joined my parents. My mother filled the bronze-embellished pots with pink tea.

Kashmiris have this peculiar habit of drinking salted pink tea after meals as it aids digestion. I disliked what we called 'Sheer Chai' and drank in small sips. Unlike me, my father relished it. After a few minutes of silence, he began with his usual questions.

'When will your so-called book finish? You need to look after your job. How many paid leaves will the company give you?' He asked, his piercing gaze not letting me off the hook. I sat in silence, staring at my teapot. In the past two months, I have applied thrice for a leave. I wanted to sit in a serene environment and write.

'I am working on it. It will make us famous; I know,' I replied with a positive but laidback demeanour. I hated locking eyes with him while communicating. His stare shook my confidence. He asked me a few questions.

'I have my book to finish,' I said to evade him. After a few more minutes, I wished them goodnight and retired to my room.

My study table was in a perfect position. I wrapped a shawl around my shoulders as I sat, looking right where the mountains stood. Only, I imagined them in the darkness and waited for the morning light to catch their glimpse. After writing a few pages, I tore them up. I had been doing that for the past three months. Pink Floyd was making its presence felt across this side of the world. Radio Kashmir was playing it at the right time. I did not look at the wall clock even once.

It was late in the night when a chilling noise startled me. A loud bang, as if of a bomb blast. We had heard rumours about such incidents in Srinagar but never witnessed anything like that. I did not pay any heed till a non-stop barrage of bullets followed.

I rushed down to the main door and saw my father outside. He was shouting expletives at what was happening around us. From the corner of my eye, I saw a group of men in combat uniforms shooting indiscriminately at everyone in their way. An unsung fear ran through my nerves. I felt, as if, something had caught hold of my spine, jerking me to come out of shock. One part of me wanted to rush out and mutilate these gun-wielding barbarians, but the other stopped me from even looking at them.

Just then, I noticed my father running towards one of them. He hit one of the gunmen from behind with a stick, making him lose his balance. Dad's heroic action brought me back to my senses. I rushed out, calling for him. As soon as I reached the spot, he started grappling with the incendiary without caring for his age or frailty.

It didn't take me long to spot the incendiary's gun. I took it in my hands and charged, shouting for my father to step aside. A fit of rage descended upon me. Seeing me approach, the gunman tried to strangle my father and use him as a human shield. I turned the gun around, gripped the barrel with both hands and, in a swift motion, landed the gun butt right on his forehead.

The sheer intensity of the blow made my father take a tumble. He landed on the side of the road. Oblivious to the other armed men firing at our neighbours, I continued beating him. I was so overwhelmed with anger that my abuses and blows on his body were in total sync.

While I was busy beating the terrorist, his accomplice entered the empty compound on the left. My father had already rushed to help our neighbour. I moved a foot or two towards where my father was when a volley of bullets pierced through my left arm. A loud shriek escaped me as I fell, motionless. One bullet had gone straight through, leaving a gaping blood-spilling hole.

'Riyaz,' my father called in a painful voice. 'Get up, my child,' he shouted helplessly as he ran towards me, stumbling on the way. I heard his desperate wail yet couldn't move an inch. The terrorist who had shot me moved on to the other houses, presuming me dead. Seeing my father rush towards me, he opened an indiscriminate fire. At that moment, life left me for a few seconds, and I felt a soul-shattering pain. I was lying motionless on the roadside, though still alive. I saw my father mowed down by bullet after bullet. The shooter smiled menacingly as he murdered my father in cold blood.

Somehow, I managed to get up, grab the gun lying on my side and shoot him. The recoil of the gun was so strong that I fell on my back. I stomped my elbows on the ground and got up again. I had enough strength left to go near him and pump bullets in his face and body. I stood there, my eyes transfixed on his trembling body. I looked for other terrorists around; I wanted to decimate them all. A second later, my legs gave in. I crouched, one hand supported by the knee and the other resting on the gun's barrel. My body felt like a fireball. I couldn't take it anymore.

My father was lying dead, his eyes fixated in the direction where I had been lying a minute back. My eyes filled with tears, but they felt dry. I felt unconditional anger towards my father's killers and everyone who had conspired for this barbaric act. At that moment, I felt someone limping his way behind my back as if trying to rise from the dead. It was the first injured incendiary. He was bleeding and crying for help. He looked at me, his eyes imploring me to spare his life.

In a swift motion of violence, I grabbed him by his head, punched him in the gut and threw him back on the ground. I held the gun between his eyes and shot him dead. His eyes looked into mine, asking for mercy, but he got none. I did not even look back as he slumped dead, leaving my face and hands bloodied forever.

The Hills Beckon

Delhi July 2019

ISBT, Kashmiri Gate, was full of people waiting for their rides. Amidst the chaos, I tried to focus. My heart was fearful, but my mind seemed prepared for the consequences. It took me a while to find my bus. I had a book to keep me company, though I did not feel like reading. My thoughts went as fast as the bus on the highway.

I recollected my mother talking about my father's frequent work trips to Himachal Pradesh. I wondered if those trips were a farce to hide something. I tried to catch some sleep as the bus cut through the empty roads. My thoughts engulfed the only framed picture of my parents that adorned our house. The stain on my father's white pashmina and my mother looking at it.

'His mangled car was retrieved from a ravine on the Chandigarh-Solan highway. No one knew why he went there,' my mother's words kept ringing in my ears. My eyes were moist; a lump started to build in my throat. I felt a sense of loss. I was trying to plan a course of action, but my judgement seemed clouded.

The bus stopped at an eatery in Punjab. I ordered chapatti and dal *makhani*. I was starving. The aroma of butter mixed with the lentils felt like a relaxant for my stressed brain. A glass of sweet buttermilk on the side filled me up, making me forget my worries for some time. I wanted to stretch my legs. It was 1.30 am. Empty stretches of land filled my gaze. The silence of the night was broken once in a while by the noise of cars and buses on the highway. I lit up a cigarette and inhaled all my thoughts. My brain heaved a sigh of relief from all the contemplation. I was ready to let myself relax until I reached Solan.

I hadn't been to the hills for a long time. I popped a pill that could help me bear the treacherous mountain passes in case altitude sickness crept in. A few minutes after boarding the bus, I closed my eyes and counted the seconds under my breath. Half an hour later, I felt my phone vibrate twice. The simultaneous vibrations indicated the delivery of an email marked important.

I tried to find my phone in the bag on my lap. When I opened the email, my body felt a sudden palpitation. The email greeted me with a 'Hello' and the contents read: 'I know you have left the national capital to find my whereabouts. Best of luck in your endeavours. Here is another one for your journey.' It ended with the same name as the sender of the birthday message–Yoginder Sharma, Solan.

The email had an attached PDF file. I opened it, and the cursive handwriting forced me to adjust my seat and sit straight. I felt breathless for a moment. *Was someone playing a game, or was this a riddle to solve?*

The content in the attachment was illegible. I had to zoom in and increase the phone's brightness. I turned towards my fellow passenger. He was moving in his seat with his eyes closed, trying to find some sleep. I read the write-up ten times at a stretch.

Why had my father written all this? Did he write this? Why, after all these years, someone had intruded into my life at such a personal level? I thought hard as questions hit my mind. I read it again to find clues that could help.

The Rebirth

1987

I cried my lungs out near my father's lifeless body, hoping my mother to be safe inside the house. A sudden urge hit me, and I got up to tend to the neighbours. My father would have expected me to do so. I carried the automatic gun with me, wary of any further threats in the area.

All around me, I saw dead bodies and their loved ones wailing beside them. All the six houses in our block lay shattered. Blood splattered all over. The melting snow on the lanes had turned red. I trembled with fear as I reached the last house, where a tragic sight awaited me.

A toddler was wailing near his dead mother's body. His arms were full of his mother's blood. He was trying to shake her and stroke her cheeks. I didn't know who saved the child from dying. Around him, I could see a bloodbath–the entire family and their bullet-riddled bodies. All I could see in his lifeless eyes was the fear of being left alone.

What would he aspire to be when he grows up? Would he seek revenge as I had already started? Would he walk the bloody path I was walking for the past fifteen minutes? I thought. I ambled towards his slight frame and placed my hand on his head.

His hand clenched his dead mother's wrist. For a second, I considered pulling him up in my arms and adopting him. But the next moment, my heart and soul snapped, and so did my index finger on the trigger. If the bullets I had pumped into the bodies of the terrorists made me bloodied forever, this one bullet altered the course of my very existence.

The bullet not only snatched that child's life but also took away my soul with it. It went right through where his heart was thumping. My body felt strangely relieved as his blood splashed my face. I was devastated, yet a changed man. I not only wanted to avenge my father's death but also the entire block of people slaughtered like animals.

With the automatic still tucked under my arms, I began a long journey that would take me to unexpected places. It would make me experience things I had never even imagined before. How a Kashmiri, working in a secured corporate job with aspirations of becoming an author, tucked an automatic gun under his arm and walked into the sunrise would be folklore for many years to come. My tired feet felt like giving in, but my spirit was undaunted. I knew the way but not the destination.

At that moment, I knew I would do something I had always refrained from. I had seen youngsters of my age taking up arms to become incendiaries. In the last year, religious fundamentalism had seeped into the entire Kashmir valley. The group of people would garland me when I would reach out to them in the ruined condition I was in; I knew for sure.

As I walked, I wondered what would become of the man who wanted to make his family famous and earn truckloads of legal money. That money would have built hospitals and schools in my peaceful village. I wondered what would happen to the book I was leaving midway and whether the title would ever make it to the bookstores.

On the Road, NH1

July 2019

'What the fuck?' I said aloud as I read the write-up for the first time. What was it all about? Did my father kill two terrorists and a child in cold blood? I asked myself unanswerable questions. To try my luck, I replied to the email. Immediately, I received an email bounce error.

It was becoming a dangerous path to tread. I read the write-up twice but refrained from reacting like I did earlier. My co-passenger was fast asleep. It was 3 am, and my eyes were strained. The mountain passes were about to begin. I felt the change in the smell of the air.

My brain could not make anything out of the two letters. The handwriting of both the posts was similar. The stories were connected, but I could not understand the reason behind sending the letters to me now. I was perplexed—who was Mr Sharma, and why he had come into my life with startling disclosures?

'You look disturbed. Is everything all right?' My co-passenger asked, pointing towards the light switched on.

'Yes, everything is fine. Sorry,' I replied, trying to put on a fake smile. I switched off the lights and looked out of the window. I tossed and turned in the seat, wanting to reach the destination sooner. The next two hours felt like hell. My gut churned, and my body felt dehydrated.

I didn't dare touch the water bottle. My head was spinning as the driver made vicious turns on the passes. I shut my eyes, gritted my teeth and clenched my fists. It was necessary to distract the mind. The task was more important and scary than the mountains.

I fell asleep and woke up at every alternate curve. The ordeal continued until we reached the city entrance. As the bus stopped at the bus stand, my body felt relaxed. My legs were aching. I couldn't wait to get down and reach the hotel. I wished the hotel had a spa for rejuvenating.

The bus stand was within walking distance from the hotel. I felt the fresh morning breeze as I walked towards the hotel. I had a quick conversation with the friendly hotel manager as I entered my room and looked around. My eyes felt sleepy and tired. The morning sun peeped through the thin curtains covering the windows.

I looked at the mountains in their early morning magnificence. For a moment, it made me forget my plan to sleep. Reluctantly, I went to bed and lay down. A peaceful sleep engulfed me within a few minutes. I was, as if, deep into an abyss for hours till a knock on the door woke me up.

Sojourn at Solan

July 2019

I had instructed the hotel manager to wake me up at 10 am by any means. He did not disappoint. My body was unwilling to get out of the deep slumber, but my heart and mind were alert with curiosity. I went to the door and received a piping hot cup of tea served in a gold-embellished kettle.

The staff knew how to wake up their guests. I looked for a pack of cigarettes. It was in my bag. The aroma of tea and cigarettes was enough to awaken my senses. I freshened up.

'It's going to be a long day,' I murmured. I tried to style my hair, looking in the mirror. My fascination with hair gels started as a teenager and continued. On my journey to unravel the truth, I was trying to look prim and proper. The breakfast was laid for the guests. The shade was perfect, and the weather was fine. As I planned the day digging into *chole bhature*, the hotel manager came up to strike up a conversation.

'Sir, if I could be of any help during your stay in town, please give me a call,' he said, handing me his visiting card.

'Sure. Thanks a lot for all that you are already doing. I like the breakfast,' I said and smiled. I also told him about my day's task—to meet old colleagues of my father and collect some photographs for his birthday gift. I told him the story with such an emotional depth that there was no way he doubted any bit of it. I shook hands with him and left for my room. The quest was about to begin.

I boarded a bus towards my first stop—a local police station on the city outskirts. A friend had arranged a meeting. My legs began shivering as the bus reached the spot, and I got down.

Will this quest leave me insane or unexpectedly satisfied? Only time would tell! I pondered. My contact was a Senior Inspector with a towering frame and a handlebar moustache. The nervousness of being in a police station was written all over my face. Senior Inspector Shikhawat greeted me warmly. The name shone brightly on his nameplate. I greeted him with, 'Hello, Sir.' He was intimidating me every second.

'You are nervous, kid. Calm yourself down. Have some water,' he said as he pointed towards the glass of water on his desk. I gulped down the water, took a deep breath and tried to settle my wandering mind before speaking.

'Thanks. I think I am sweating because I am not used to being in a police station.'

'No one is really used to being here except for us uniform-clad, so-called patriots. Anyway, what brings you to this small town? I heard from Ajay that you needed some help.' Ajay was a senior at the office. He was the one person I trusted completely, be it with my work or a suggestion on any personal matter.

I told the SI about receiving the letter and email with the write-ups seemingly written by my father. He got puzzled for a moment but started smiling the next. He asked me if I was serious about going after someone based on a letter and an email that gave no clues. The way he asked me was discouraging. I looked around, trying to find an answer.

'I think I will try to find the address, Sir,' I said, looking into his eyes. I was serious about it, and he could see the determination on my face.

'It could end up leading you nowhere; keep that in mind. Plus, I won't be able to help you officially as this is not a police-related matter.'

'I will be glad if you will guide me even unofficially,' I replied.

'Let's go out and have a smoke.' He instantly got up from his seat and asked me to follow him. Outside the police station, there was an area for car parking as well as recreation. Some chairs had been set up within the shade. He took out his Four Square and lit it up. I stood there, thinking if I should light up mine.

'You don't want to smoke here? I can see you have a pack in your jeans pocket,' he said with an intrusive, questioning look and smiled. I was carrying a Classic pack. For the next few minutes, there was an eerie silence as we both looked at the heavenly mountains while smoking.

We discussed a few plans to trace the sender of the letter. I wasn't sure of the plans he laid out before me. Nevertheless, I listened and noted them. I was hopeful I might get lucky the next day. SI Shikhawat asked me to wait outside the gate. He wanted to show me around the city. I had no choice but to oblige.

The second day began on a similar note as the first. A sumptuous breakfast filled my soul with the best spirits. It helped me prepare for the grind through the day. I read the contents of the letter and the email once again to look for clues. Yet again, it proved futile.

My thoughts went to the second person I was going to meet. I was hopeful as compared to the previous evening. The state administration and the people occupying the big chairs were powerful enough to find out the truth behind any conspiracy.

The meeting, which I had thought would be beneficial, finished in less than 15 minutes on a disappointing note. The private assistant in the District Magistrate's office laughed at my story and did not even allow me to have a word with his boss. The cards I had thought would help me in this game had fallen out badly. It was embarrassing.

It was around noon when I left the DM's office with

no fixed plan or destination. I pondered about my next course of action.

Should I use the post office plan suggested by the SI yesterday, I wondered as I stopped at a nearby restaurant. *Or, should I approach the cyber-crime cell or an ethical hacker?* I wasn't sure if these would help me in my quest. I tried calling a few friends in Delhi and Mumbai to get me in touch with anyone with contacts in Solan but to no avail.

I sat for the next one hour at the restaurant, chalking out a plan, but decided to go sightseeing instead. The sun was shining bright, but the chill of the mountains had a profound effect during this time of the day as well. I called the hotel manager. With his help and guidance from the locals, I took a shared vehicle to a serene hill spot. Even though my mind was still in turmoil, the picturesque location had a calming effect.

The splash of the waterfall on the hills gave my mind a new wave of thoughts. I had been trying to find a person who maybe did not exist. I knew I had no chance of tracking the email but the letter could help. I was hopeful. I wanted to track down the post offices.

Being a small town, I expected the number to be limited. However, there was a pain point. I had no idea how many post boxes there were in the town.

Downtown, Srinagar

The calming effect of the scenic waterfall and the hills lasted only till dinner. Half an hour after retiring to my room, I received another email, sending traumatic signals to my brain.

'Looks like you are trying to be an investigator in Solan. You are taking giant strides. I can't wish you any further luck. If you work hard and are lucky, you will definitely find me. Till then, read this.'

My eyes looked for the attachment, which had the same cursive handwriting. This game was troubling my mind more than ever.

Thirty-seven days back, I came to downtown Srinagar with nothing but my broken body. My soul wanted to embrace revenge. I had to know every detail about the shooting, but for that, I needed to sacrifice everything that I stood for. Getting arms training here was impossible, but making contacts was probably the easiest.

I knew only one man would help me in this quest—my maternal uncle. With his help, I met some of the most famous names in the jihadi circles. The local mujahedin was in charge, while the external sources had started clawing inside the minds and psyche of the men here.

Sometimes, I wondered what I was doing, wasting my life in this rotten hell, but the heart wants what it wants. No one here knew about the masterminds behind the shooting that shook the lives of everyone in our tiny hamlet. I had no idea where my mother was. Was she dead or still grieving for my father? I kept asking questions to myself as a comrade walked past me.

'What are you writing?' He asked.

'Nothing important, just trying to jot down a few poems flooding my mind,' I replied.

He did not understand even a word of what I spoke or wrote. He said I thought deeper than he could comprehend. He also believed I thought too much about the shooting, and instead, I should let it all go and kill the traitors around me.

'Killing gives mental peace, my brother,' he rejoiced as he said these words.

A few minutes later, he left, leaving me alone in the cocoon of my lonely existence. I wondered how long it would take to unravel the mystery I had set my sights on. I was lost in thoughts as I tried to find the long-lost friend of mine, a bottle of rum that had kept me company for the last week.

I usually drank with the other comrades in the evening, but today was the first time I had poured myself a drink while the sun was still out. We always ate and laughed wholeheartedly when we drank together. We weren't allowed to grieve for the ones we had left behind.

We were not supposed to show our emotions, for we were brothers-in-arms against tyranny. Somehow, today, I felt like bursting my own bubble of emotions and drowning in the realms of intoxication. Would these words ever see the light of day outside the valley? I wondered as I cried silently, praying for my mother to be safe.

***

I hadn't written for a long time. The comrades had been asking me about my writing habits, and today I wrote after ensuring everyone had dozed off. I had kept my diary a secret, but I didn't know if I could keep it hidden any longer. My training had already begun, and by the end of this month, I might head to the camps where they make experts out of us.

Hey Almighty! I beg your mercy. I had been making new friends, and a source told me that the perpetrators of the barbarism orchestrated in my village happened to be the training experts in these camps. I was looking forward to seeing their faces. I was going to make them pay for what they did to me.

The Mystery of Mr Sharma

July 2019

The latest write-up made me uncomfortable. My mind was having different perceptions about the man I had seen, although rarely, for the first two years of my life.

'Should I follow these write-ups or not?' I asked myself yet again. I felt weak. Would I be able to show all these letters to my mum? I had already been going through an existential crisis since crossing twenty-five, but this was utter madness, something that I had never experienced before. Was I up for this task?

The next morning, I woke up with a fresh start and headed out. I had to be strong—for myself, for my mother and for that one man whose truth I owed at least to my heart. My target was the nearest post offices. I had to sweet-talk someone at the post office to know if it was even remotely possible to get any information about the letters.

It took me an insane amount of cajoling before a postman finally agreed to help me. He was a man who knew about the whole town, having delivered letters across the length and breadth of the town for twenty years.

'Are you going to help me just by looking at the letter?' I asked him as he was busy staring at the letter I had received. His poker face gave nothing away as he kept reading intently.

'I am not sure if I can help you, but we can definitely try. There are not many Mr Sharma's in this town. Should we start from the nearest?' He asked for suggestions.

'Take me wherever you want, Sir. I want to find the man who has turned my life into a mystery.' I was ready to make any effort to find closure. My spirit needed a raging fire, and the postman here was the spark. He asked me to meet him outside Lane 15 in the old part of the town the next afternoon. He wanted to finish his duties before commencing this detective act.

I was excited. I spent the latter part of the evening loitering around the hotel area. During the dinner at the hotel, I had a hearty chat with the manager. We discussed local politics and businesses. At the back of my mind, a thought lingered. *Would I get a sound sleep tonight or a new write-up?*

It kept me wondering what life was or is for the one man I wanted to know everything about. Later, in my room, I organised all the write-ups I had received and began reading from the first one. I wanted to find a connection as soon as possible. Else, I knew I wouldn't be able to sleep.

While in Delhi, I found one write-up we received at home years back. It was on my external hard disk. I arranged the printouts as per their received date. It was my first tryst with my father's writing.

Work-Life (Im)Balance

1990

Part 1

The last three months had been the most excruciatingly stressful months of my life. Juggling between work and the upcoming responsibility of being a father had started to take a toll on my mind and body. Writing it down here helped me relieve the stress. My boss had been after my life to take an overseas project, and I had been making excuses to avoid it.

I hadn't yet revealed my family life to him. I couldn't, I was afraid they would sack me or probably try to harm my family. For them, work was paramount. None of them had any emotional attachment to their respective families. Sometimes, I wondered how they even faked it when they talked to their loved ones.

Whenever I felt overworked or let down in life, I ended up getting depressed. Whiskey and poetry were my only saviours. It would be a gross injustice if I didn't write my thoughts in this diary. I had been longing to fill up the diary with my thoughts. All I had to do was open these pages and go through them.

All the pain and depression vanished from my life. I hoped someday, my child would read my thoughts and make good use of them.

This one I wrote for all the amazing women I know:

'Their passion for life makes your eyes take a turn. With their vision and passion, all problems do burn.

The mere mention of them brings an unmatched glee, for when they are around, the sadness does flee.'

This one was written when my mind was full of questions, and I was introspecting strongly for the answers and found some:

'Do you gaze in the wintery sky?
When the stars are shining, the moon is not shy.
Do you walk in the chilly winds?
When the legs give up, the soul wants to cry.
Do you run, afraid of the dark?
When the breeze touches you, the noise flies by.
Do you live this thing called life?
When you fall all day long, yet stand up to try.'

Part 2

It had been three months since my family got complete. The birth of my son made me a little more vulnerable, but it also made me protective. I was more afraid than ever, but I continued with my work wholeheartedly. It was indeed a challenge to keep looking over your shoulder in the constant fear of someone harming you.

I had been to three foreign assignments in the last seven months and got myself almost killed twice. The sole purpose of my fighting against the odds had been the will to keep my family safe. Although there were no dangers, I knew they would break down if something happened to me. Yet again, I felt like filling the diary with what I had in my heart and mind.

The Search Continues

July 2019

I fell asleep with the printouts lying around me. I woke up early in the morning to the rustic sounds of birds and the fresh air that only a mountain town could possess. The day was going to be long and the evening harder. I sat on the bed looking at the mountains, wondering about the life of my father he had written of.

How would he send this out to someone who was posting it to my address thirty years later? How did he hide it all from the family if everything written in these posts was true? Was he really hiding a secret all the time behind his intense eyes?

I began asking myself questions, trying to remember my last memory of him. The memory was blurred, with all the focus on his eyes. I closed my eyes and tried to dwell deep into my memories until someone from the room service broke my reverie.

The mountains always have an early morning, and I had to wait for the postman at the hotel until late afternoon. Taking advantage of the time I had, I forwarded the contents of the received emails to a few of my friends who had contacts with cyber security analysts. Though I was not expecting them to wave a magic wand and tell me the sender's address, I did not want to leave any stone unturned.

I had told the postman the name of the hotel I was staying in. As expected, he was on time. We started walking uphill and reached a cluster of houses. He signalled at the red-coloured bungalow to be our first quest. The nameplate read 'Sharma's,' and I felt an upswing in my heartbeat.

We went to three houses that evening but ended up being disappointed. Who was that Mr Sharma who knew about our lives inside out? I wondered. I thanked the postman and took his leave after having some tea nearby. He told me that if he recollected any other Sharma around this area, he would drop in directly at the hotel or call.

All my hopes had already started dwindling. I had come on a mission that seemed to have failed even before kicking off. I started to realise that I could not find the truth behind this secret without getting obsessed with it and leaving everything I had in my life. Was I even ready for that? I questioned myself.

The urgent four-day leave at work was to end soon, and the barrage of calls and questions from the clients was to start. Was my work more important than finding the truth about my father? I began questioning my actions while I had three cups of tea and a few cigarettes.

All these four days, I had told my mother that I was on an official trip and would be mostly busy. Though I was not incommunicado, I was not keen on revealing anything to her until I found something. As the smoke of the cigarettes rose, I saw faint hope. The woman I did not want to share anything with could help me at least get a start.

This whole mystery was numbing my mind and leaving me breathless. I wondered how she would react when I told her of these things or questioned about my father. I hadn't had a heartfelt conversation with her about Dad since I left home to live in a hostel during college.

Return Journey

July 2019

During my return bus journey, I felt so crestfallen that I slept from tiredness. I had no strength to think about what I had been trying to achieve for the last few days. Upon reaching Delhi, I resolved to solve the mystery by hook or crook. I decided to talk about this whole episode with my mother. Over the next two days, I worked half-heartedly at the office.

I went to my hometown to see my mother. The decision proved to be the best in my life. As usual, a full breakfast awaited me as soon as I stepped in. The peculiar relationship between a mother feeding her kids and the kid always being leaner than he was earlier couldn't be comprehended. It was something that we all had tried to understand but failed.

The strictness from the teaching career of almost three decades had affected her personal life long back. As a child, she would remind me of my responsibilities by narrating stories about how she quashed her dreams of being a national-level athlete and instead chose a stable life for her child's upbringing.

Later in the day, while having tea, I casually asked Mum if she knew any Yoginder Sharma from Solan, who was my father's friend. As soon as she heard my words, her face lost its colour. She was standing and quickly held on to a chair for support. I felt as if her heartbeat increased exponentially. She kept looking at me.

'Yes, I do. However, it is not a person. Instead, it's a code used between your father and his maternal uncle. I have something that mentions this name,' she said and stopped. 'I am curious; how and what do you know about Mr Sharma?' she quickly asked, narrowing her eyes as if scrutinising me.

I assured her I would tell her everything in detail, but she would need to cooperate with me. She agreed. I could sense she was hesitant. I told her about the letters, emails, and PDF documents. She was shocked. I refrained from telling her about my travel to Solan.

She asked me to show her the letters and the emails. I obliged. She confirmed my father's handwriting in the PDF documents. I could see her eyes swell up with emotions, but she controlled herself. In her bedroom, she opened the wardrobe and took out an old vanity box.

It was the vanity from her marriage and had a small cavity at the bottom. As a child, I had seen the box many times but never knew it could hold something private.

From the cavity, she pulled out some documents. They were handwritten posts, I could sense from a diary, my father's diary, to be precise. Feeling overwhelmed, I gathered my thoughts and started reading.

Everything seemed connected with the posts I had received. Mum sensed my emotions building up. She asked me to take the papers and read them later at a convenient time. By mentioning Mr Sharma and my father, I had touched a painful nerve. I had to stop myself from discussing further on this topic and continued random conversations with her.

She asked me about any friends and if I had found a special someone to spend my life with. I was least interested in such random talks but had to play along. I didn't want her to feel troubled later when I returned to Delhi. Later that night, I decided to read the handwritten notes alone.

Get Married, Please

September 1988

Every morning, I prayed to God to give me the strength to face this life. The transition had been drastic. Going from a family man to a battle-hardened wanderer wasn't a part of my wildest dreams. Destiny brought forth unquestionable circumstances in life. After almost a year in the wilderness, I returned to my village.

I kept tabs on my mother through various informers, but going to meet her in daylight meant a direct threat to her and my life. She had sent me a message last week through one of these informers, asking me to meet her as soon as possible. I decided to meet her after her dinner.

The moon was shining bright, and the demonic silence on the roads made my mind return to that horrible night a year ago. The night that changed my path kept returning like a nightmare. As I walked past the houses that were pierced open by bullets, I felt a drop of sweat trickling down my forehead across my left eye.

The pleasant weather of September had given way to a slight chill at night. I was wearing a brown fur jacket. I was carrying a Berretta automatic, just in case. Discreetly, I entered the house compound. I hit the wooden knocker on the door twice in quick succession, just as I always did. My mother had received the news of my arrival, but she did not know when I would come.

As soon as she saw me at the door, her teary eyes welled up, and she held me in the tightest of embraces. Many kisses and hugs later, she asked me about my well-being. She quickly went inside the kitchen and brought the bronze teapots and kettle. She poured two cups of Kehwa tea, and, for a moment, I forgot what I was.

My heart and soul felt filled to the brim with love and care. The way she looked at me without speaking made me want to forget my revenge and move on to ordinary life like before. She tried talking about Abba but stopped as soon as I looked at her with bloodshot eyes.

She knew I was thirsty for blood, and I didn't want to talk about him. I had been after the orchestrators of that attack for almost a year and yet was unsuccessful. I directly asked her about the reason she called me here.

'I am dying,' she said with a straight face. I kept looking at her as my physical strength diminished suddenly. I kept the teapot down. I thought I did not know fear. Here was God showing me that even the worst barbarians can be fearful at times. Not for their own selves, but for someone who was their own. I went near her and held her by her shoulders.

'What is happening?' I asked her.

'I have high blood pressure. The doctor has told me that there is a huge risk to my life. I need you to help me by doing me a favour.'

'What kind of favour, Maa?'

'I know you won't agree, but I want to see you married and return to normal life before I shut my eyes forever. I don't want you to be on a newspaper headline as a martyr or a jihadi or whatever they call it. You can take your revenge in some other manner, but please come back. Those bastards will kill you like they killed your father and countless others. I laid him to rest a year back; I don't have enough strength to cry over your dead body.'

'You won't need to. I can take care of myself.'

'I know you can, but Zeba, your maternal aunt, has found a young girl who can take care of you as well as me. Only if you agree.'

'Which girl?'

'She recently represented the state in a shooting competition. Please listen to me. Leave all this behind and marry her. I will speak to your uncle and arrange something for you outside Kashmir.'

Jahangir's Kehwa

January 1989

The snowfall had started a week back. Despite the weather, I decided to venture into a local teashop on the highway in South Kashmir. I wanted some Kehwa. It was late afternoon, and I was having pangs for tea all day long. Jahangir made the best tea in the area, and its aroma used to satiate me. That was all I needed on this wintery day.

I didn't know that a tall, handsome local had been sitting there since morning, waiting for me. His jacket was immaculate, and shoes were polished. He looked like a high-ranking officer in CBI but for his curly, unkempt hair.

I observed him at the corner table as I went to Jahangir behind the bill counter. We exchanged greetings. I asked him for a cup of tea.

'At your service, Sir,' he gleefully replied. I had taken a few sips of the tea and was starting to relish the bread when I saw the stranger approach my table. I had an uncanny

feeling but didn't want to give anything away.

'Hi, Riyaz, how are you? Is it true that Jahangir serves the best tea in Kashmir?' He asked, pointing at the tea.

'I am fine. Jahangir is a gem, and the Kehwa is always out of the world. Do we know each other?' I replied.

'Not yet. However, we quickly need to. By the end of this year, we both will need each other more than ever,' he replied, leaving me in a trance. I had multiple questions coming up in my mind but refrained from speaking much.

'What do you mean?' I asked, keeping my questions crisp and to the point.

'To be precise, I know everything about you since your childhood. I know what your mission is. Someone wants to help you accomplish it. The question is–are you willing to do the hard yards, or do you want to keep living in the bubble that you have been in for the last year or so?'

As soon as he said these lines, I instinctively got up to leave. I did not want anyone or anything to mess up my thought process. I didn't want anyone to interfere with my mission. I kept my teapot aside and moved a step away from the table.

He placed his hand on my left hand and caught hold with a grip like that of a trained army man. The grip made me remember my maternal uncle. I looked at the stranger with a soft face and saw his eyes light up with fire.

'Mr Bhat sends his regards. I hope this grip makes you remember your uncle.' I froze as he remarked about my uncle.

Who the hell is this guy? I thought to myself. I kept

staring at him for a few seconds until he finally spoke again.

'I have been sent by him. He has already spoken to your mother about arranging to get you back into the mainstream. Whatever we talk about should remain between us, and not even your mother is allowed to know a thing,' he spoke softly. All I could manage was an affirmative nod. I was in a state of shock and didn't know how to react.

'Bhat Saab will get in touch with you. Look out for telegrams from Yoginder Sharma,' he said, got up, and left, leaving me in a deluge of unanswered questions.

New Delhi

1990

I looked at her sombre eyes and wondered if she was happy. Six months had passed since we got married, and I had spent most of it on the road. I had requested my handler to give me internal postings in Delhi, where we lived, but luck was never forthcoming in this business. I was sleeping beside her, feeling the deepest contentment I had ever felt. The cold weather of Delhi was spreading its wings during the night.

I felt like smoking, but she held me so tight that I did not even try to move an inch. Sleeping in her arms was heavenly, but looking into her eyes while making love was eternally blissful. I was in love with her, but was she equally in love with me? I pondered as sleep evaded me.

She adored me, but was this her real calling? Was this what she always wanted to do? I began questioning myself, knowing that I would never get her answer to any of those. Her real persona was uncovered only in front of me, but I felt there was more to her than what I knew.

I had hidden my real line of work. Probably, that's why I was getting paranoid about her, as well. With the comrades, months used to pass idling around. Here I was, overthinking everything that was a part of my life. I had cut myself out of the ordinary living routine while in the company of the comrades, and adjusting back had made my mind all fucked up.

I remembered how shy and silent I was when I first met her. She was the one talking while I was only contemplating whether to talk about my business. I was projected as a Central government employee in the marriage biodata and boy, did I look like one! Hiding in jungles had made me so good at acting that I could easily pass off as a middle-class, nine-to-six working man, living each day only to achieve the targets.

Reaction

July 2019

The mention of Kashmir in the posts evoked mixed emotions in me. The rational in me had always castigated Kashmiris for what happened with Kashmiri Pandits in 1990. Most of the moderate Muslims who did not side with the extremists had to flee as well. On the other hand, the pragmatic in me was willing to go there once and see whether the place lived up to the hype everyone talked about so consciously.

I was engrossed in the posts I had in front of me. I was about to pick up the posts again but stopped for a second. I had many questions, and the only person to satisfy my curiosity was sleeping. I decided to ask her everything in the morning.

'When did you get to know about all this?' I asked her. We were sipping our morning tea while the birds outside chirped away in a steady rhythm.

'To be honest, I didn't know anything till you were born. Some weeks after you were born, he began to feed me information, things I could not believe. It has been twenty-eight years since our lives changed, but I still don't know the complete truth. These diary entries are just a part of a bigger story, something that remains untold.'

'I want to know the truth. There must be a reason I have received these letters and files. Someone out there wants both of us to know the truth.'

'I don't want you in any danger. Please think about it,' she replied in a concerned tone.

'You don't need to think too much, Mum. I am not doing anything adventurous. I just want to find this Sharma guy and know the real story.'

'Find Bhat Saab. He lives in South Kashmir, in the middle of a terror hotspot. However, I cannot let you go there. That man took my husband away from me; I can't let him take you away.'

'But Dad suffered an accident. Didn't he?'

'Yes, he did, for the world. In my heart, I know, and still feel, he couldn't have died behind a car steering wheel. It had to be a conspiracy.'

'You are thinking too much; just breathe.' I used my go-to statement of breathing, just like I always used when someone's emotions seemed to get the better of them. I never learned how to handle an emotional person.

'I am fine,' she replied.

'So, it wasn't an accident, according to you?'

'No, definitely not. Someone conspired to have him

murdered and displayed it as an accident.'

'You always believed this, yet you never tried to find the facts. I wonder why.'

'All of us were too broken to investigate anything. We just accepted what we saw,' she said, slightly teary-eyed. I quickly went and gave her a tight hug. I had already made up my mind. Nothing was going to stop me from finding the truth. My father's memory deserved a just ending; I had started to believe.

The two important people who could help me find the truth were without their first names. It was going to be tougher than going to Solan. Looking at my excitement and confidence, Mum was tensed.

'You will have to call me regularly from there, whenever you go. Do you understand?' She thundered all of a sudden with red eyes.

'Yes, I will do that,' I replied, as softly as possible.

'Can you call Mr Bhat and inform him about me wanting to visit Kashmir?'

'I don't have his number, but I can get one of our relatives, Zeba Ji, to inform him. She lives in Kashmir. It will be easier for her.'

'Great. I love you, Maa. By the way, who is Zeba Ji? Why haven't we met her ever?'

'She is your father's maternal aunt.'

I asked her if she believed the diary entries were sent to her by Mr Bhat or someone else. She was clueless. She told me that she received these posts a year after Riyaz's demise and had kept them hidden.

Goal Setting

August 2019

There were certain things that I had to accomplish before I set out on the weirdest journey of my life. I knew it could be a make-or-break type adventure and I was willing to risk it all. I decided to take a flight from Delhi to Srinagar but later thought about the cravings of my soul.

How sad it would have been if I had not experienced the mountains and streams via the road. I booked a flight to Jammu and a cab from the airport to Srinagar. It took me an hour to finalise everything. The tour operator seemed friendly during our conversation.

I went to my office to meet the reporting manager. I requested a month of leave. I was fine with leave without pay, but it was tough to convince them of a long absence from work. The wanderer, as he used to call me, wasn't going to be a good enough excuse for this. I mixed some facts and told him about the trip to Kashmir.

'I have to look into the sale of an ancestral land,' I told him. He did not ask any further questions and agreed instantly.

I also had to meet Neha and tell her about my plan. She was the rock based upon whom I had found a new purpose in life over the last year. I couldn't leave her out of my decision to go on a quest that could even spell doom for my mental stability. I asked her to meet at our favourite hangout for a coffee.

Over the last six months, we had seen the place blossom into a quaint café. I reached the café and ordered my default black coffee with some cookies to munch on. She was stuck in traffic. As soon as she entered the café, my heart skipped a beat like always. The smile was as immaculate as I had last seen, full of warmth. We had our usual gossip about office life, and later, I told her my plan in detail. She was the one who had always inspired me to seek the truth.

'I feel so proud of you. Wish I could go with you and help in any way possible,' she said.

'Thanks. I know. Actually, I feel nervous going alone, but I feel it is my calling.'

'I hope you find out everything you want and return safe and sound.'

'Hope is the only medicine I carry,' I replied. I was to leave for Srinagar after two days.

Dal Lake

August 2019

I stayed at The Lake Resort on Boulevard Road. The hotel room overlooked the majestic Dal Lake. Nehru Park radiated in the middle of Dal. The morning view of Dal Lake was not so silent after all. The breeze was hitting the mind and body with full vigour. I had been in Srinagar for the last two days and was slowly getting acclimatised to the environment. I paced forward on the Boulevard.

'Your father would have been proud today had he been alive,' a deep baritone voice spoke from behind me as I quickly turned around. A burly man, well built, not more than sixty, was standing with a confidence that could challenge a 20-year-old youngster. His overflowing white beard drew me towards him. His eyes had a sort of magic. As soon as he stepped forward to give me a quick hug, I regained my senses and paid my respects.

'Namaskar. *Waray chukka*?' He asked if I was all right, in fluent Kashmiri. He also inquired about my mother and everyone in the family.

How come I don't know this man while he knew everything and everyone in my family? I wondered. I was falling short of words talking to him.

'You are totally like your father. An absolute introvert till the time you open up,' he said, as I kept quiet. I hardly knew anything about my father to respond.

'I had the best time of my life with him. He wasn't just my sister's son. He was more than a friend.' He went on as I listened with all my attention. I had to know everything from him. Every word and moment that he could recollect.

'He was my best protégé, and that's why I need to take it upon myself to enlighten you. Your father was not a full-time civil engineer as you have been told,' he said, and I almost broke into a nervous fit. My brain cells were waiting for the next words. The world woven around me for thirty years was about to take a turn towards the actual truth.

'I have worked with many army officers, intelligence sleuths, terrorists, and terror sympathisers, among others. I have known many brave soldiers who are ready to kill or die for their causes and beliefs. In addition, I have seen leaders who inspire an entire generation to follow them blindly.

'However, to tell you the truth, I haven't met a man or a woman as remarkable as your father. He is the bravest man I have ever met or worked with.' His eyes gleamed with pride as he finished speaking, giving me enough reasons to believe his words. My body felt numb, listening to him. I waited for a few seconds, thinking he might resume.

'Aren't you going to reveal the complete story?' I asked, looking at him with childlike eagerness. I had come all the way to Kashmir for enlightenment, and I wasn't willing to be left disappointed.

'I will, son. I will also show you the overflowing emotions in each word he had written,' he replied.

'You mean the diary?' I asked.

'Yes, the diary of a star. My star and yours, as well.'

'The star that watches over all of us,' I remarked and saw the old man smiling with tears in his eyes. He gave me a tight hug and told me he had been carrying the weight of my father's story on his shoulders for many years.

'You mean even my mother doesn't know the truth?' I asked.

'No, only half of it. There were so many things that your father couldn't tell her.'

'Why?'

'There were a lot of details that couldn't be known by anyone outside the agency.'

'Do I get to know about that as well?' I asked.

'You will have to wait, son. Patience is the key. You shall get to know things at an appropriate time,' he replied and paused. His phone started ringing, and he excused himself to step away.

'Are you crazy?' He shouted on the phone. His face turned red with anger. 'I don't understand this shit. Who advised them to go ahead with this? Am I a useless pig sitting here?' He started walking around while talking on the phone. It seemed something had transpired, and he despised it. I didn't know what was happening. He came to me after disconnecting the call.

'Go back to your hotel. I will contact you via the hotel reception. The Indian government is planning something drastic for Kashmir. Be safe, please,' he said. His words were rushed. Nervousness was written all over his body language.

'You already know which hotel I am staying in?' I asked calmly.

'I know everything,' he replied and went towards the lake area. I tried to observe his movements. He hitched a ride with someone on a scooter.

This guy is mysterious, I thought to myself as I followed his advice and returned to my room. I was so overwhelmed that I didn't even ask about the letter and the emails. I was sure that this man had sent them. No one else knew so much about my father.

Article 370

August 2019

The rush of people around the lake had decreased by the evening. There was a rumour going around that the Indian establishment in New Delhi had decided to change the future of Kashmir. I overheard the hotel visitors and staff talking about urgent meetings organised in many areas of Srinagar. I wanted to enjoy a boat ride but could not book one. I decided to have dinner at Aahad restaurant. The *Wazwaan* was mouth-watering. I was so engrossed in the delicious food that I paid no heed to the news. Suddenly, a strange commotion started in the restaurant; the people started going to each other's tables.

Hushed-up conversations followed as I momentarily lifted my eyes to check the TV. The faces of the locals around turned red. They were staring at the TV screen. The channels were breaking the news of the house arrest of all the Kashmiri politicians. There was a crackdown on the separatists. There were reports that the Indian army had sent 60,000 troops to the valley. The situation was about to turn ballistic.

'Oh, lord, which hotel are you staying in?' The manager came near me and asked in a state of shock.

'I am putting up nearby. Don't worry.'

'Please hurry up. We need to down the shutters in ten minutes. The situation is not good.' He went to all the tables.

Am I a Kashmiri who could never call this place home? I wondered as I brought the fried lamb ribs, commonly called *Kabargah,* towards myself. I closed my eyes as my tongue tasted the mutton cooked in milk and fried in ghee. I wanted to cherish the moment as much as possible.

Here I was–alone in Kashmir, having delicious food amidst reports of a crackdown and an impending assault. Better sense prevailed, and I quickly finished my meal. I felt satiated at last. The hotel was a ten-minute walk from the restaurant. On my way back, I saw soldiers setting up barricades around the area.

I tried to message a friend who was a journalist in New Delhi. Within seconds, I realised the mobile signal had disappeared. Life over the next few days was going to be more than just tough. I quickly went to the hotel and asked the manager to help arrange a call via his landline.

I wanted to call my mother and inform her about the situation. She was bound to get worried. I was late. The landlines were disconnected as well. I wondered about the actual motto. I felt at the mercy of an uncertain life for the first time. As I went into my room and switched on the TV, I was shocked.

The cable television shut down, and the only channel working was DD National. Was this an immaculate plan of the government before taking a big step, or was the establishment taking Kashmir to ancient times? I went downstairs and inquired with the manager. He told me that Article 370 was about to be abolished, and all the anonymity held by Kashmiris was going to be lost.

I felt gloom overtaking me as two other men joined us. They discussed the disadvantages of such a drastic step. I acted as a silent listener. After a while, I asked them if they saw even one advantage of this step. None of them answered as they looked at me with suspicious eyes. They tried diverging from the question by bringing in other topics.

They started ranting about Muslims being selectively thrown out of the valley. I knew whatever they were imagining was just a figment of an incorrect thought process. We kept discussing for an hour and then went to our respective rooms. The manager was a local, but he decided to sleep in the hotel.

He wasn't sure he would be allowed to reach his home downtown. I quickly charted my course of action for the next day. I wanted to go around the area on foot and check the situation first-hand. I had no faith in the media and the gossip.

6th August 2019

The next morning shocked everyone associated with Jammu and Kashmir. Srinagar was under curfew. Section 144 was imposed in both Jammu and Ladakh for maintaining law and order. In India, even the government couldn't take anything for granted, let alone the ordinary people.

I couldn't move out of my hotel. The food and water supplies at the hotel were enough to last a week. As the people of Jammu and Kashmir were coming to make sense of this new order, the Home Minister got a Presidential order and proceeded with presenting the same in the Parliament.

The people in Kashmir started planning to protest. They had been throwing stones at the armed forces for decades now, with or without a reason. This time, the clampdown was so strict that people were picked from their homes and detained. The Central government put leaders, separatists and many influential people under house arrest.

There were rumours that some people were taken to

jail in Agra. Not a single bullet was shot in the next two days. The mobs were dispersed with pellet guns, injuring some protestors in the process. The CRPF was showing restraint, and the J&K police were going about their duties in the bravest way possible.

The threat of terrorist exigency loomed, yet they stood their ground bravely. The locals seemed aghast at this move. They were complaining about the atrocities of the armed forces. I didn't know whom to trust. The communication was restricted to the local market in the lanes that I visited stealthily during the evening hours. On the evening of 7 August, I received a note at the hotel reception. It was from Bhat Saab.

'Tomorrow 5.30. Be ready.'

It came as a sign of relief. My quest had to reach a logical conclusion, and Mr Bhat was the only source. In addition, I wished to see the surreal beauty of Kashmir. That night, I didn't sleep properly. I felt excited when I received a call on the room extension.

'Uncle is here,' the manager said.

Was this the start of my journey towards enlightenment? I wondered as I grabbed my bag to head out.

'How did it feel spending two days in a literal jail?' Uncle asked with a smile as I reached him. He looked sleep-deprived but still had the same charismatic aura.

'Not too bad,' I replied and quickly jumped into the Gypsy. My mind went back to the story about my father's new Gypsy. The Gypsy that he was driving on the day of his accident.

'Did you learn anything?'

'Yes, two things. One, there are two or three different perspectives on the same situation. Second, we can't trust anyone.'

'Atta boy! Like father, like son!' He exclaimed as the Gypsy turned a corner. The fresh air of the morning engulfed my senses. The pollution-free sky looked serene as the silence on the roads broke with a rare hawker or pickets of CRPF.

'Was this step necessary?' I asked without even looking at him.

'Not really. We will be sure once we get the results. The restrictions might continue for a month or two, but that shouldn't stop us. We have a goal to chase.'

'Care to explain more?'

'Peace in Kashmir is my only goal.'

'Yes, true. I have a different goal as well, to know the truth.'

'You will, eventually. Everyone does,' he replied and continued driving.

'Can I drive?' I asked suddenly and left him startled. I wanted my best dreams to come true. Not many things compare with driving an open Gypsy on these mountain passes.

'Yes, sure. We will stop for tea at a nearby place. From there on, you can take the wheel.' He told me we were headed to his home in South Kashmir. An hour later, we stopped at Gulshan Dhaba. He said this was the only tea stall open on the highway. The owner enjoyed special privileges from the elite in the Indian Intelligence and the paramilitary forces. I wondered how.

'This guy serves the best *Kehwa* and omelette in Kashmir,' he said as we got down, welcomed by a middle-aged man. They both exchanged pleasantries while we sat at a table overlooking a ridge. The omelette was spicy, and the tea was out of this world. My body felt awakened.

'Are you headed home, boss?' the shop owner asked Uncle while maintaining a stoic silence.

'Yes. He wants to see the paradise of South Kashmir,' Uncle said and pointed towards me. I smiled meekly as my eyes met the shop owner's.

'Welcome to the lost paradise. May you achieve what your father couldn't,' he said, leaving me in a trance. I looked at him and Uncle. I wanted to ask him how he knew Dad but restrained myself. As we continued our journey further, I started driving. I felt Uncle was a little relaxed as he soaked in the serenity of the surroundings.

'Have you spoken to Zubeida?' He asked and looked at me. I stared at him for a second with the I-don't-know-what-you-are-talking-about look. 'I meant your mother. We sometimes call her Zubeida,' he said.

'No, I haven't spoken to her since the day before. The network is dead.'

'We will speak to her once we reach my place.'

'How is your phone working?' I asked. He looked at me and smiled.

'If they cut the connection to my phone, they might as well lose Kashmir.' His words left another ball of haze for my mind to negotiate. I was concentrating on my driving. I applied brakes for a millisecond and looked at him. He continued smiling. I was in awe. My mind was busy establishing a connection between him, the tea stall owner and my father.

'Children these days learn so fast,' he said.

'Children have a lot of questions as well,' I replied.

'They shouldn't hesitate to ask.'

He told me about the extensive spy establishment in Kashmir. Boat owners, tea stall owners, bus drivers, police officers, unemployed youth and bureaucrats–everyone was a part of the circle. Jahangir, the owner of Gulshan Dhaba, was an integral part of the agency and had been with them since the 1980s.

I felt connected to my roots as we crossed small towns and villages. The lush greenery around was so enticing that I wanted to forget about the world outside the valley. The small huts in the middle of nowhere, rivulets flowing down, and the enormous pine trees made it a scene apt for a movie shoot.

Two days in this part of the country made me realise what I was missing for thirty years. I cursed my luck every time someone spoke about Kashmir; now, I was cursing my life altogether. I had possibly missed what could have been the best years of my life.

'Did the film industry shoot the movies this side?' I asked him.

'Not much. Pahalgam and Gulmarg have always been their favourites.'

'Why?'

'They were developed and proclaimed as tourist hubs. The majority still prefer those two places. They have a shikara ride in Dal and feel Kashmir is over. Anantnag, Mattan and Verinag in South Kashmir have been the star attractions for the locals. Even Bandipora could have been a tourist hub. Some foreigners do visit for a trek or an adventure.'

'Which area do you like the most?'

'My personal favourite is the Aru valley,' he said after a pause.

'Never heard of it. Will I get a chance to visit?'

'Do you like trekking and camping?'

'I don't mind.'

'Mind you, everything is shut down as of now. You might have to camp alone.'

'That's fine.'

'Good. Then, you will definitely get a chance to visit.' I felt elated as he said this. I wanted to explore the places where my family had spent their formative years. He started pointing out and naming different villages as we drove further. I had never felt this relaxed driving through a hilly terrain.

My emotions were swelling, but the morning air kept a leash on them. People were standing outside their houses, talking to their neighbours. The newspaper vendors and milk delivery people were missing. Abrogation of Article 370 had shut down the heart and soul of the city and the villages. There were check posts everywhere. Paramilitary was on the roads. Amidst all this, our vehicle was not stopped even once.

'That bungalow on the hill belongs to the ex-Chief Minister,' he said, pointing to a grey-coloured house protected on three sides by the security agencies. The hills in its backdrop looked magnificent.

'Wow. It looks like a palace,' I said, already lost in pristine thoughts.

Uncle's House, Anantnag

8 August 2019

The stream of water flowing adjacent to his house sent a gentle breeze across the rooms. The snow-capped mountains looked majestic from the windows. I wished I had more time in my life to explore them. The aura of the landscape was such that for a fleeting moment, I contemplated settling there.

South Kashmir has been facing terrorism in its worst form since 1989. Yet the barbarism, bullets and bloodshed of the innocent weren't able to take away the natural splendour. Anyone from our parent's generation would agree that South Kashmir was the most beautiful part of Kashmir.

The waterfalls and lush green surroundings with pine trees added to the marvel. Long before the terrorists made this area their operations hub, the locals used to come here for picnics. Days were spent looking at the mountains without a care about the world. The serenity played a major part in maintaining the interest among people.

Possibly, the imbibed calmness was the reason the Kashmiri Pandits never took to guns, even after being overthrown from their homeland. They were harassed with announcements from mosques at night. Mutilated, raped, and killed in scores, yet they never let their inculcated values betray them. I was standing near the first-floor balcony with these thoughts in my mind. A persistent noise from the other room jolted me back to the present.

It seems Uncle has some visitors. I thought to myself. After listening carefully for ten seconds, I realised the voices were coming from a recording.

'Is that my father's voice?' I asked, having tiptoed to the other room. I didn't want to disturb him.

'Yes,' he replied, staring at me as if searching for something. This man had such intensity in his eyes that merely looking at them made me anxious. The recording was of a man shouting instructions to multiple people. After listening for the next five minutes, I understood in detail about the conversation. It was indeed my father leading a group of terrorists.

I learned from Uncle that he led a group of ten to fifteen mercenaries into Kashmir every month. He was the man trusted with the life of multiple men by the organisation's bosses. Uncle told me about the operations my father handled in Kupwara, Budgam, and even the southern areas of Kashmir, like Anantnag.

'But why didn't our army, BSF or J&K police catch him?' I interrupted.

'Because he was our man,' he replied, pausing the CD player.

'He was helping the terrorists infiltrate into our areas, and yet he was our man. What sort of conspiracy was this?' I asked.

'All the men that came here with him were listed down as soon as they arrived. Our agencies put a marker on each one of them. Almost all of them were neutralised within a year. Except for one bastard,' he replied. The doubts that had crept into my mind began to see some light. My father was living a double life.

The thought of him as a path bearer for the terrorists shattered me. The other life was to help our security agencies identify the rogue elements and pin them down. My mind was bursting with questions about everything.

'Who is the bastard you are talking about? Did he get away or something?' I asked. Uncle approached me and held my hands. I felt he was about to cry when he said something that pierced my bones with a poisonous dagger.

'That man was the reason your father left us so soon.' It felt as if a rock was placed over my shoulders. The lump in my throat was growing into a monster with each passing second. My body felt let down.

'But my father died in a car accident,' I said, with a heavy, choked voice.

'Yes, he did. Sometimes, what meets the eye is not the complete truth. The accident had many details, which the police ignored. Our team investigated for a month and found the truth,' he replied. I slumped further into the wooden chair I was sitting in.

'His friends survived, but he couldn't. Is that what led you to believe it was a conspiracy?' I asked. As a child, when I heard the story, even I had questions about how the others survived.

'Yes. Indeed, your father was too brilliant a man to die in a car accident. He was trained to survive even a burning car. He had once come out unscathed from a truck fallen in a gorge. He could swim underwater, holding his breath for minutes. He sustained third-degree torture and yet survived. His mental capability and endurance were the best our agency had ever seen.

'It is possible that having lost your grandfather made him that tough. Yet he never gave away the secret. He used to talk about his emotionally unavailable nature and his ability to shut himself down when the situation demanded.' Uncle paused and smiled. The pride of working with such a man made his eyes gleam.

'You know, we felt he was like a child who could be moulded into any form we liked. After he completed three operations, we surprisingly found that he was like hardened concrete. We used to water him with information, and he got us results,' Uncle continued lavishing praises on my father.

The feeling of intimidation was turning into

admiration. The respect I had in my heart for my dad was increasing. *Why didn't my family know the real story?* I started to wonder. If I had known the truth about my father, would I still be here as an engineer, or would I have chosen a different path, something related to security? I questioned myself. Uncle went towards the kitchen. He wanted to have water. His throat was parched, having spoken too much.

His Real Life

August 2019

I intended to know every detail of my father's life, most of which was a secret to me. I asked Mr Bhat if he could tell me everything from the beginning. The intimidation had the better of me.

'It was after your grandfather's murder that night in 1987. Your father wanted to be a literature czar but he became something else. The part of his diary at your home consists of some of his poems, but his life was much more than that,' he said.

'I don't think he stopped writing even after drifting from the mainstream middle class.'

'No, he didn't. Unfortunately, most of his stuff was lost. Some of his write-ups are safe with me. They are not for the world to see.'

'Am I a part of that world?'

'You, my son, deserve to know every detail.'

'I have many questions.'

'Shoot.'

'Did he actually become a terrorist?' I asked.

'He just walked away from home and contacted me for help to infiltrate extremist groups. He had promised me that he would return home soon, but he didn't for a year. Your grandmother sent me a message seeking help. I sent some of my best men to find him. He was living in the jungles. He was trying to trace the footsteps of the two mercenaries who had bloodied his village. When I saw him, I literally broke down. He wanted revenge, but it was tough to catch the conspirators sitting across the border.'

'Did my grandmother agree to your suggestion of him working with you?'

'No, she didn't. She was a doting mother. She was concerned about her son's safety. We convinced Riyaz to leave everything around February 1989. We wanted him to marry and settle down. The thought of him working with my team didn't arise till a month later when he disappeared again.'

'Seriously?'

'Yes. He killed a terrorist handler with his bare hands. His range of informants in South Kashmir was brilliant. He received a tip-off that Altaf had arranged the logistics for that fateful night in 1987. He confronted Altaf outside a local bakery. I was told that an AK-47 was found lying next to Altaf. Police arrested Riyaz, but my boys got him released. I retrieved him myself from the Anantnag Police Station. His eyes were so calm that I thought he was in shock. Later, I realised we had unearthed the Kohinoor of the intelligence world.'

'Isn't calling him Kohinoor the biggest compliment?'

'We killed more than a hundred terrorists with his help and were able to neutralise some over-ground workers as well. All this within a span of two years. I believe if he had survived the accident, we would have been able to wipe out the roots of terrorism in Kashmir in three or four years.'

'He surely wasn't your only asset. You could have wiped out the terror with the help of others.'

'A local Kashmiri is your biggest asset. Kashmir, as a whole, is a mystery box. You never get the real flavour till you peel one layer after the other.'

'Have you ever reached the last layer?'

'Sorry?'

'Have you tasted the complete flavour?'

'No one has. Not even this old uncle of yours.'

'How many years did you serve in the intelligence?'

'I am still serving,' he replied, and yet another wave of shock went through my nerves. I felt drops of sweat trickle down my brow. It took me five seconds to come back to reality.

'That's really cool. All this spy action and thrill. Isn't it adventurous?' I asked with a smile. I was behaving like an adolescent who had met his childhood-favourite uncle. He just smiled.

'I am not important. We are here to discuss your father. Let's not diverge from the real hero,' he replied after a pause.

'Ok. So why didn't any of your other assets work as he did?' I began again.

'Haven't you understood till now?'

'No.'

'He was the best. No one in Kashmir valley had his level of relationships.'

'Didn't you recruit the other locals who lived here?'

'We recruited the locals as well, but they didn't gain our trust. Something or the other always happened. A major terrorist would slip away from our hands. In one famous case of a slip-up, two dreaded bomb experts fled from the police station. They were responsible for setting a shrine on fire some years later.'

'Basically, the local population revolted against your teams.'

'Precisely. They were brainwashed to be revolutionaries. Religious fundamentalism had its most dangerous decade in Kashmir till 1998.'

'Did my father help in changing the scenario in any way?'

'You can say he played his part at the onset. After his demise, terrorism grew exponentially. He knew we had to chip away at pieces to unravel the actual puzzle.'

'How many years have you been living here?'

'For an eternity,' he replied and paused for a moment. 'I am the Kashmir expert for the Indian bureaucracy. They come to me whenever a problem arises.' He spoke in such a measured tone that I could not fathom the pressure he must have been feeling. His responsibility was much bigger than I could ever imagine. To be the man in charge of the crown needed guts of the highest degree.

With the same poise, he went towards the staircase. He opened a small door and entered a storeroom. The room was full of books. A wardrobe was engraved on the wall. I took a few steps towards the stairs and saw the wardrobe, full of papers. A smaller wardrobe and a sturdy chair also occupied the room.

'Finding your father's work is going to be a task. Do you mind helping?' He asked politely.

'I would love to help.'

'But you are not supposed to read the details in the other documents.'

'Sure. I won't,' I replied, excited.

Over the next hour, we rummaged through endless papers. I read some documents by mistake and some deliberately. Some of them made no sense, while a few gave me an insight into the world of Kashmir diplomacy. The ones related to the supposed remuneration for the separatists gave me a jolt.

There were photocopies of FIRs and signed surrenders of certain terrorists. Uncle's house was a gold mine of secrets. A week or two here, and I could gain real knowledge about this region. Finally, Uncle stumbled upon the neatly folded pages and the cursive handwriting. He carefully took out the papers and handed them to me.

'Make him proud.'

'I will try my best.'

Father's Diary

August 2019

After having lunch, Uncle asked me to play the CD and told me to listen carefully. The tape had my father's voice in a hushed tone.

'Why did he record this audio of instructions? Was he training others to be like him?'

'Yes. Absolutely.'

'Did he succeed?'

'Partially. We expected too much from him I guess.'

'Can I copy the contents of this onto my phone? You won't mind, right?'

'Please go ahead. This is your property. You have all the rights to do as you please.'

'Are there details of any operations listed in these pages and this audio?' I asked. I wanted to get closer to the truth of his life.

'They were never documented. I can tell you about

some of his famous works. He hasn't glorified anything in his writings. His modesty was unparalleled,' he replied.

'Please tell me more,' I said. I was excited.

'Should I begin with the last operation he commanded?'

'Ok, sure.'

'It was code-named Operation Lidder.'

'You mean after Lidder river?'

'Yes, precisely.'

'Tell me more.'

'It was the only mission your father failed in,' he said and paused. His voice was full of sorrow and disbelief.

'The mission gave away his cover, and then he left our team. After that, your family was threatened multiple times, but he faced everything bravely. Till that fateful evening, when he left us all,' Uncle said and started to sob. I went near him and gave him a glass of water. He stared silently out of the window at the mountains. The pristine calmness soothed his nerves for a second before he began to breathe heavily. He looked troubled.

'Are you all right?' I asked. I was standing near him, hand on his shoulder, trying to comfort him.

'Never been better,' he replied with a smile. He wiped his tears off, gulped down the water and began narrating the tale of truth.

'The operation was botched up due to a high-ranking State government official. Riyaz was a non-state agent; he was a part of both sides. The terrorists aimed to spread mayhem all across the Kashmir valley. They wanted to cause floods in the Lidder using explosions. It could have destroyed the harmony in the farmer community.

'Jhelum and Dal were also the targets for a similar operation. If they had succeeded, Kashmir would havc suffered for generations. It would have destroyed the apple orchards, the magnificent Dal Lake, the saffron grown in Pampore, Aru Valley, Pahalgam and the entire farming sector in South Kashmir.

'Riyaz got a whiff of the plans near the end of 1989. We both were working on ideas for controlling this menace. We knew the mercenaries wanted blood, but it was new. During the same time, the exodus of the Kashmiri Pandits had started. Our work was disturbed because of the chaos.

'We somehow managed to stop the terror threat, but we could not stop your father's cover from being blown. They got to know his line of action and came after him like hungry beasts. We had to get him out of Kashmir.'

The details of my father's life proved too much for me to bear. I felt as if the verge of breaking down was nearing.

'Who ratted him out?' I asked with a choked voice. My eyes were fixated on my feet.

'The personal assistant of the Minister.'

'What the fuck? Did he get punished for the crime?'

'No, people in power don't get punished. Besides, ratting someone out is not considered a crime in this country as per the political convenience.'

'Do you think that other high-level politicians were also involved?'

'I have my reasons to think in that direction.'

'If you teach me how to shoot, I would like to murder all those responsible for my father's death,' I said. My eyes were on fire; my heart felt determined.

'Hold your horses, son. This is not a movie. Real life doesn't allow us the liberty to take drastic actions like this. That man died five years back. You are not killing anyone without any reason.'

'I have a reason which is bigger than my mediocre life.'

'Really? Are you sure you want to walk on that path of revenge? The path your father once trod upon and, as a result, spent his last year in regret.'

'Why not? If that means removing a few parasites from this country. It will definitely improve our internal security.'

'If you walk this talk, I am sure Riyaz's heart will swell with pride wherever he is.'

'Will you give me an opportunity?'

'I will send you for a trip up the hills. You will get your chances. It will be upon you to grab them.'

Mission Report

August 2019

Later that evening, upon inquiring further, Bhat Saab told me about my father's missions in J&K. He also shed light on some operations my father conducted in New Delhi and Punjab, which were instrumental in flushing out some sleeper cells working against the Indian establishment in 1990.

He also spilled some secrets, like how my father kept his injury hidden from everyone, including the team and the family. Something in the stories was creating a deep bond between us.

'He was a patriot. A complete son of the soil who lived and died with his conscience clear,' he said and I kept staring at him, lost in thought. I secretly wished for a chance to emulate him.

'Did he avenge my grandfather's brutal killing?' I asked with a heavy heart.

'Oh, yes, he did. Ten times over. He got that entire group. The perpetrators, planners, handlers, and the ones who supplied arms. He didn't kill them together, but he got them all.'

'Did he feel proud, or good after that?'

'No, he used to puke at the mere thought of killing anyone.'

'Yet he did.'

'Absolutely. Sometimes, you have to have an ambition that you can serve with a far greater responsibility than anything else in your life,' Uncle said, and I began pondering if I had any such ambition. Was I willing to risk everything, even my life, to find the truth about my father?

'What are you thinking? Don't be too harsh on yourself. Your father was a great man. You have the whole life in front of you.'

'I'm not being harsh on myself. I am wondering if I would get a chance to do even one per cent of the work he did for our nation.'

'I'm sure you will. But first, do you want to serve your motherland, Kashmir?'

'Yes, I do,' I replied instantly.

'Take a light dinner tonight and enough rest. If you need medicine to induce rest, I have a cupboard full of it. You can choose.' He signalled towards the bar cabinet, and called out his servant. He got us two glasses and a bottle of twelve-year-old Dalmore. The evening had set in, and the breeze was already getting the better of me.

As I took the first sip of scotch, I contemplated about the next day and the adventures that might startle my ordinary life. The beauty of South Kashmir was creating ripples in my eyes. My brain marvelled at the thought of having spent my childhood in such an area.

Would I have been an entirely different human being? I wondered as the night inched closer. I didn't get even a second of sleep that night. The morning sun and the chirping of birds gave me tremendous energy. I was ready to face the odds.

Trekking Near Lidder

9 August 2019

Early the next morning, I was ready to go camping on the banks of Lidder. The river got its name from a place called Lidderwat, near the Aru Valley. The approach from Anantnag was mesmerising. Although my body was in trauma due to altitude sickness, I stared open-mouthed at the natural beauty.

Missing the medicine had its perils. I was hoping that I didn't puke in the car. Half an hour into the journey, I completely forgot about my sickness. The passes were so beautiful that I clicked pictures after every turn. It was a magical sight for my already besotted eyes.

The mountains and the orchards opposite the campsite sparkled. The sound of the flowing water and the gentle breeze calmed me down. I could feel peace in all directions. My overthinking mind deserved some rest. The guide helped me set up the tent and provided the required essentials. I sat near the riverbed, feeling the wet rocks for some time, when I heard someone approaching.

'Winter is early this time,' the guide said as he came closer.

'Indeed,' I replied. August was never considered a month of chills in this part of the world.

'Where are you from?' He asked, trying to start a conversation. He was standing on my right, and I was engrossed in staring at the hills.

'Delhi,' I replied, not looking into his eyes. I wanted to give a disinterested look. I was specifically instructed to not make any banter.

'Do you need some smokes or food?'

'I have my own stuff. Thanks.' I went and rested in the tent for a while. Half an hour later, I laid out the breakfast I had got. Uncle's cook had packed enough stuff to keep me full for two days. I read for a while, procrastinating about the mountains. After lunch, I decided to ask the guide to set up a place amongst the rocks.

After lighting a cigarette and feeling the drags, I lay down and fell asleep on the rocks. I had never been so close to nature, and it felt heavenly. The guide woke me up and came with Maggi and tea an hour later. The sun was moving across the horizon. It was five in the evening. I decided to take a stroll around the site. He told me that a bonfire would be set up around six. I had an hour to move around and soak in the evening air.

As I moved forward, I felt a familiar fragrance

coming from the other end of the campsite. *Someone was smoking. Would they be generous enough to share with me?* I wondered as a man with shoulder-length hair walked out. He had a round, Lennon-style glasses on him. I would have categorised him as a hippie had I not seen the tattoo on his left wrist. The multi-coloured trident shone bright.

'Viktor!' I exclaimed. I couldn't control my excitement. It had been years since I last saw him during the graduation farewell party. He looked at me but didn't react. Instead, he kept walking, oblivious to everything around, the joint pressed slightly between his lips. The smoke surrounding him was filling the whole area with its aroma.

As he passed, I tilted my neck a little to get a good look at him. He didn't utter a word, and it felt peculiar. I had probably mistaken him for my friend, and this man was actually a foreigner. I gathered my thoughts and moved ahead.

The guide served dinner in the garden. At the other end, three people were huddled together, including Viktor. I wondered how visitors were allowed at the camp amidst the lockdown. Probably, like me, they were here on behalf of someone as high up as Mr Bhat. They were busy in an animated discussion.

My eyes met Viktor's. I smiled but received no response.

How was it possible? Was my mind playing tricks? I started doubting my memory and myself. Probably, this person was just a doppelganger. A few hours later, with sleep evading me, I opened my mind bender–the bottle of scotch, an eighteen-year-old beauty. I sat outside the tent. As the alcohol was settling in, I felt someone near my tent, but as I looked back, there was no one in sight.

The silence and the sound of the river gave an eerie feeling. I decided to call it a day and entered the tent. My eyes instantly fell upon a piece of paper carefully placed near my luggage.

Meet on the hiking trail at 15.86/2.79°. Come alone. On top of the paper was a digital compass.

I woke up quite early the next morning. After having a light breakfast of fresh fruits, I spoke to the guide about the trek route. He gave me the required directions and told me the other three visitors had also left for the same route.

I started after an hour and ensured that I wasn't being followed. I kept looking over my shoulder and in all directions while going uphill. Two hours later, I was at the location.

'Was this a joke?' I questioned myself. There was no one in sight. I didn't even remember the way I came from. The next moment, the compass came to life with a green light and rang a loud alarm, which echoed around the area.

Viktor emerged from the woods two minutes later. A scarf covered his face and head, but I knew his walking style too well. His green eyes sparkled in the sun. He came and embraced me.

'Hope you are all right,' he said quickly.

'Yes, I am fine. Why are you acting strange?' I asked. I wasn't able to understand his behaviour in the camp.

'We need to be careful. They have their ears and eyes everywhere.'

'Who are they?' I asked, utterly confused.

'Hasn't the boss briefed you about your role here?'

'What the hell? I am camping here. I am not playing any role.' I was shocked.

'Oh yes, you are. You don't know yet.'

'Enlighten me.'

'The security of the entire northern region is in your hands. Rest, I will let you know at the appropriate time,' he replied.

'I hate this bullshit. For the last two weeks, life has been playing mystery games with me. I feel that Mr Bhat is the protagonist. Are you the antagonist?' I spoke. Viktor started laughing. His laughter echoed in the mountains.

'You are the bravest man I have ever met,' he replied, ruffling my hair as if to encourage me. His words sent another wave of intense shock up and down my spine. Mr Bhat had said the exact same words about my father, and here I was in the same area that witnessed my father's last act of unparalleled bravery. I was worried.

'Do you care to explain this?' I asked softly.

'I am here on a secret mission. From now on, we both are in the same team. Mr Bhat is our leader, and we take direct orders from him. Is that clear?'

'What the fuck? I am not a part of any team. Bhat

Uncle didn't tell me anything. I don't believe you.'

'It's good that you don't. Your first test will begin as soon as I leave. You will face a life-and-death situation. My role here is to prepare you.'

'Is this a joke? I don't know how to fight. Moreover, how will I survive? I am not my father. Hasn't Bhat Uncle told you this?'

'He has told me everything. Moreover, I have known you since college. I know your abilities better than he does. In addition, you have the audio on your phone. The one Mr Bhat gave you. Right?'

'Have you been keeping an eye on me?'

'I am the Assistant Director of Intelligence in Kashmir. It's my job to identify a potentially natural sleuth,' he replied. I stared at him as if the clouds had exploded with an unexpected thunder.

Am I living in a fantasy world? I thought, looking at the mountains far away. For the next two hours, Viktor brainstormed with me about the different survival methods. He made me listen to Dad's audio and discussed complicated situations.

'I will show you my automatic revolver, but remember, you won't get to fire a shot. You need to learn to survive without a weapon with you,' he said as he carefully explained each part of the weapon and other guns. We discussed the geography of the trek route and the various methods of hiding in a forest.

After a few hours, he bid me goodbye, wished me luck and returned on the same path he came from. I decided to move forward on the trek route, lost in thoughts. Viktor was a staunch Christian whom I had first met at the college fresher's party. He was the only one from our batch who had no qualms about indulging in whatever our seniors told us to do.

It was an adventure for him, as he often told me. He enjoyed the attention, especially from the females. He was not so frank but wasn't cranky, either. Over four years, I grew up appreciating him for his dedication to his trade and his drinking capacity. He used to stand up for his friends and loved ones with all his might.

Many of our coursemates used to pass out while drinking because they were confident that Viktor would help them reach their beds. He was the friend that each of us wanted. His grades were always average, like mine, and that helped strengthen our bond. We used to study and party together, along with Samar and Faiz.

Our group was the secular gang in the college. In our hostel, we were feared as the four-men hell in a cell. Our rooms always felt like a wrestling ring. All of us were fans of WWE and used to watch it with an unmatched fervour. Jumping from one bed to another was our forte, and slamming others down was a guilty pleasure.

Viktor was a proper gentleman when it came to interacting with the ladies. With him, all of us started interacting more with the females in the college. He was the *yaaron ka yaar* (people's person) all these years, but I always found one thing strange about him–he rarely spoke about his parents and his hometown.

It seemed they didn't exist for him. The rest of us used to be thrilled when any discussion veered towards our hometown, but not him. He used to avoid any questions we had about his family. Little did I know that after ten years, I would see him again on the most exceptional journey of my life, the journey to seek the truth of my family. After the last year of college, all of us started working in different directions. We lost touch, and even the advent of social media didn't help our cause. I never expected to see him until I saw the lanky frame at the camp in Aru Valley. The trek that was about to change my life forever.

Test

August 2019

Bang! A loud noise echoed. A second later, there was one more. Instantly, I realised these were gunshots. I hid for cover behind a tree. I felt the bullets coming from different directions as I tried to decide my way out. I tried to retrace my steps. A 7.62 mm round whizzed past the tree and struck the trunk opposite me. It left me shivering.

My legs were trembling with fear. I started crawling on all fours towards the set of trees ahead. They were denser and offered better cover. My heart was thumping as I heard people running in my direction.

'Where are you, infidel?' They shouted in unison as I tried to fit myself behind a tree. I turned my sight towards all directions, seeking a stone or any object to retaliate.

'Come out, you scared crow,' they shouted again and started laughing. I rolled myself to go towards another tree and had a good look at them. They were tall, wearing

Pathan suits with headgear covering their faces. The assault rifles were resting on their shoulders. I noticed an area going downhill on my left.

My only chance of surviving was to run away. My mother's face flashed in front of my eyes as I tried to gather my thoughts. I started running, first towards the north and then the valley downhill. They shot a few more bullets at me, but luck was on my side. I was able to run away from their range.

My clothes were soiled. My body was full of cuts and scratches, and my face looked messy. I rolled towards a tree and banged my ankle against a huge boulder. Tears ran down my face; it felt as if my foot had torn apart.

I recollected the audio recording I had heard at Uncle's house. 'Either retaliate with everything you got or run away,' my father had yelled at the people he was training. I wasn't in a position to react, or fight back. I moved forward, constantly looking over my shoulder for voices or footsteps. The magnanimous forest and the trees hid the shining sun. I had never felt fear of this measure.

Was I getting ready for the things to come up in the future? I wondered.

I was shivering yet steady as a voice rang in my ears. 'What do you do when you fall into a dump? Don't you wait till you garner enough strength to get up?' The audio recording was beginning to make sense. I located a ditch at the far end of the hills overlooking the valley downwards.

I took slow and constant steps towards my

destination. I wanted to hide till the sun went down. The only advantage I had was a head start of some minutes. The trekking rucksack was still on my shoulders. My body was feeling low because of the heavy weight. It was my only chance to make it through the night.

The situation felt straight out of a bad dream as I started pondering about other options. In the ditch, I carefully spread out a cover and lay down for a while. I was exhausted and famished. A bottle of water and a pack of biscuits in my bag helped me energise, but the battle was only half won.

The evening and the night in the forest were going to be long and tough. For a second, I thought of going in the direction of the attackers but then decided against it. The evening was getting colder with each passing minute. I lay inside the ditch, hidden by some dry grass.

Before coming for this trek, I had researched about this area and was sure wild animals would come calling soon. I had to find myself a safe spot. I waited for approximately an hour at the same place. I went up the hill to ensure that the miscreants had left the area. The area had such dense trees that it was impossible to see beyond a few meters.

I decided to pitch my tent between two trees. It was dangerous to spend the night on the ground. After carefully tying a rope with multiple knots between two trees, I entangled the rope with the camping tent. It was a lesson learned directly from the videos of adventure-seeking backpackers.

The floating camp became a reality in thirty minutes, and I heaved a sigh of relief. The circumstances were teaching me to utilise my skills. As a wise man rightly said, 'It's all within us. We just have to reach out for it.' It was beginning to make sense now, but I wasn't sure if I really was the chosen one, as Viktor had said.

I dipped biscuits in the water container and ate them slowly. The idea was to keep myself light yet energised in case of any eventuality. The bottle of whisky was confined to the bag, for I wanted to stay alert. The moonlight shining through the dense trees felt brilliant, and the glittery stars reassured me that the world wasn't coming to an end. Feeling the cold, I began to rub my palms and feet. Within ten minutes, I fell asleep.

Post Trek Morning

11 August 2019

The next morning, I decided to retrace my steps and head back to Anantnag from Aru Valley. I deliberately avoided the main roads and instead trekked through the forest areas. I stopped in my tracks twice because a leopard was keeping a constant watch on me. I did not want to mess with the animals in the wild. It was their area, and people, like me, were intruding.

The river flowing downstream was cold as I washed my hands and face. The icy cold water provided an instant freshness. My mind was struggling to comprehend the attack of the previous day. I was wondering if there was any clue Viktor left me with, to contemplate further actions. I didn't even have his number or any way to contact him.

Should I go back to Anantnag and see Mr Bhat? I questioned myself as I heard a military convoy pass. I was walking on the stretch that was nearest to the main road. I waved at the last two vehicles. The vehicles passed me and came to a screeching halt fifty meters ahead of me.

Four men came out of the two vehicles and pointed their automatic rifles at my face. I slowly raised my hands and fell down on my knees. I had seen such situations in the movies but never imagined myself doing it.

'Identify yourself,' shouted one of the men in uniform.

'It's in my bag,' I said meekly. My physical strength had deserted hours ago and my mental strength was getting depleted exponentially.

'Shut up and show us an ID. Are you a recruit?' He asked.

'Hold on, Captain. I think I know this guy.' A civilian, wearing khaki trousers and a camouflage jacket, jumped out of one of the vehicles ahead and came towards us.

'What? Who is he?' The man in uniform shot back.

'I guess, he's an author from New Delhi. Not sure what the hell he is doing here.'

'Author? Really? He looks shabby enough to pass by as a beggar.'

'I know, but he is. My colleagues covered him once for an interview.'

'Ok. Let's bring him in. Will you take his responsibility?'

'Yes, sure,' he said and began to move towards me with the Captain and two soldiers. One of the soldiers picked up my bag and began to search. The Captain and the civilian lifted me and helped me towards the Gypsy. They gave me water and an orange.

'His name is Raheel Dar,' the soldier said as he closed the back door and went towards the other vehicle. I was slowly peeling off the layers of orange.

'Let's take him home,' the Captain ordered. The civilian seated in front of me calmly took the bottle from my hand. He asked me to chew the orange slowly. My body and mind were not reacting. I was beyond tired.

'I am Varun Pokhriyal. I work for the M-news,' he said softly. I gave a wry smile. The Gypsy started moving and I felt puckish.

'Can I just lie down?' I asked in a measured tone, not to alarm him.

'Please go ahead. Do you want anything else?'

'Some peaceful sleep,' I replied.

'This is Kashmir, buddy. Sleep is never peaceful in this part of the world,' Captain shouted. He was sitting in the front passenger seat. Varun smiled and signalled me to lie down. His eyes looked reassuring.

Journey to an Army Camp

We reached the army camp in thirty minutes. The guards at the gate inquired about my identity, but Varun and the Captain managed somehow. My mind was looking for a bed to crash on. The hanging sleep in the customised tent at night had caused a blistering pain in my lower back.

I felt a limp while walking. They accompanied me to the mess and offered breakfast. Captain asked me if I wanted tea or coffee alongside.

'If you allow me to sleep for some time then,' I replied.

'You can sleep after a small briefing with the unit leader.'

'Really? What will I be telling the leader, Sir?'

'That's upon you and him. It's out of my pay grade,' he replied and handed me a cup of coffee.

'Do you guys drink it neat?' I asked, and he started

smiling. He signalled with his head, and I got his answer. The box of sugar was lying on the table behind us. Coffee cheered me up a little. He sat next to me, shook my shoulders and told me not to doze off. We started talking about my trek and the route I had taken from Aru Valley towards Pahalgam. I didn't tell him anything about my encounter with the armed mercenaries.

I wasn't sure if they were terrorists or anyone from the security agencies. I lied and told him I had to sleep in the forest because I lost my way back on the trek. He wanted to know the details of my visit to Kashmir, but I refrained from telling him the truth.

Bhat Uncle, Viktor, and the truth about my father were my secrets, and my conscience didn't allow me to reveal anything about them. He was eyeing me with suspicion and was about to ask another question when Varun joined us. He picked a plate of breakfast and sat on the chair opposite mine.

'Should I get you some tea?' I asked. I wanted to avoid Captain's inquisitions.

'No, it's ok. I will get it,' he replied.

'Our author friend seems to be fresh now,' Captain Sharma cut in.

'Your zeal is rubbing on me, Captain.'

'In that case, are you fully prepared for the briefing?'

'Oh, I thought I was briefing you. Is there one more?'

'You have been questioning him?' Varun asked, glancing curiously at Captain Sharma.

'Not really. I was just having a friendly banter about

his visit to Kashmir,' he replied, looking at me for affirmation.

'Don't try to mess with me, Captain. I know a lie when I see one,' Varun retorted.

'Yeah, lies have a special connection with you. For the record, I wasn't even questioning him. You can ask him if he felt threatened.'

'Yes, we were just discussing my trip to Kashmir,' I cut in. I had a feeling that these two highly egoistic individuals would do anything to undermine the other. I didn't want the situation to get out of hand. They had helped me out of goodwill, and I owed them. I asked them to relax and got up to get some tea from the counter. As I approached the counter, there were two soldiers ahead of me. One of them was a Major.

He inquired about my identity and the purpose of the visit. I told him about the camp, trekking locations and the story of me losing my path while returning from Pahalgam to Aru Valley in the passes. He inquired further about how I was still on a trek while the entire state was under lockdown.

I told him that my mobile had been dead for three days and I had left for the trek four days back. Going by his behaviour, it seemed that he believed me. He told me that he was the unit leader. I heaved a sigh of relief. Maybe this was the last interrogative session I would have to face, I thought.

When I returned ten minutes later with tea, Varun and Captain Sharma were discussing something animatedly.

'I thought you had found a tent to sleep. So much time for two cups of tea,' Captain Sharma said aloud as I was nearing their table. Varun turned towards me and smiled.

'We are lucky that we have been brought our next round. Aren't we, Cap?' He jumped in.

'Yes, extremely lucky. It saved me from the briefing I had to attend later.'

'You met Major Anand. Is it?' Captain Sharma asked.

'Yes, Sir,' I replied, pointing at the Major sitting five tables away.

'How did it go?' Varun asked quickly.

'It was fine. A few questions asked. Appropriate answers given. So far, so good,' I replied.

'That's great,' Captain said.

'Can I get a bed to crash on for some time? I really need a shut eye.'

'Should I show him to my tent?' Varun asked, looking at Captain Sharma.

'Sure. Let's go,' he replied. All of us got up together. As we moved towards his tent, my mind was filled with thoughts and images of the previous day. The sound of bullets whizzing past my ears was troubling me endlessly. I realised I might not be able to sleep in this condition, but wanted to try it. It was important to take care of the exhaustion.

Conversation with Varun

'Looking at your battered condition, I don't believe that you were on a trek,' Varun said suddenly, jolting me out of my thoughts.

'But that's the truth,' I replied, not looking directly into his eyes.

'You shouldn't lie to a lawyer, doctor, and journalist. They look right through your lies. Didn't they teach you in your training?'

'What training? By the way, I am telling the truth.' He was making me nervous with each question. If he could look through my story, the army officers would have surely started a check on my past whereabouts in Kashmir.

'I know who you are, Raheel. I am fully aware of your background and your family history. I didn't say anything in front of Captain to avoid you from getting into trouble. The army isn't lenient when it comes to complexity,' Varun said, leaving me shocked.

I came to Kashmir to find the truth about my life and family, and here was a guy who already knew things about me. Was this a hunch he was playing? I decided to play the game his way to test the waters.

'Looks like you know more about me. Please enlighten this poor soul,' I replied.

'Your father was a spy. Basically, a double agent.'

'Really? Are you sure?'

'Yes, absolutely. I have had endless cups of tea with Mr Bhat. I can confirm one thing–do not take that man at face value. Most of his words and work have motives unseen by mortals like us.'

'What's that supposed to mean? Who is Mr Bhat?'

'The man who, most probably, sent you on that trek. You shouldn't trust him.'

'OK. What else do you know about him and my father?'

'Your father was a true patriot. He was the best agent India ever had. His death was not an accident but a conspiracy.'

'Bhat Uncle has already told me these things.' I realised there was no point hiding anything. I had to believe him.

'When did you meet him last?'

'Do I have to answer all your questions?'

'Yes. I am the only one who can help you.'

'How will you help me? You don't even know my aim of being here.'

'You are here to seek closure. You want to know about your father and his legacy,' he said, leaving me weak in my knees. He either had supernatural powers, or his connections were so powerful that I had to succumb in front of him.

'Yes, you are correct. I met him three days back. He took me to his place.'

'Wow. That place is a goldmine of information. What did he tell you?'

'Stories about my father. About his role in Operation Lidder. About the conspiracy around his accident.'

'What is Operation Lidder?' He asked.

'Some operation that Bhat Uncle led along with my father in 1989. About poisoning the Lidder and the irrigation system at that time.'

'OK, go on.'

'He told me how both of them, along with their men, were able to eliminate the conspirators and complete the operation successfully.'

'That's interesting. You might not know, but there has never been such an operation in the valley.'

'But he told me that the chief conspirators of that operation were not neutralised, and they were the ones who planned my father's assassination.'

'Are you serious?'

'Why? Do you think otherwise?'

'Yes, I don't agree with this version. His accident was orchestrated by the Indian establishment, probably ordered by Mr Bhat himself. In addition, there was no Operation Lidder in 1988-89. There is one, which has been under process for the last year. And because there was no such operation, the whole story has been fabricated by him.'

'Why should I believe you? Moreover, why would he fabricate a story?'

'I will help you with the proof and eyewitness accounts. You will have to give me some days for that. Moreover, you are the son of probably the best spy Kashmir ever had. Bhat Saab stands to gain a lot. You, on the other hand, might lose everything.'

'Do you know Viktor?'

'He is the AD of Intelligence in the Valley. Why?'

'My battered condition is because of him.'

'Tell me more,' he said. He narrowed his eyes down and looked at me with suspicion.

'No, I won't. I will not reveal anything else till you get me something substantial. You might be playing me and just gathering information.'

'Ha ha. You have serious trust issues. We both have things to share.'

'True. Let's help each other. Although I don't know what you gain from it.'

'I want the truth to see the light of the day and not buried forever.'

'How do you know the reason for my visit to Kashmir?'

'I will answer when you do.'

Evacuation

11 August

Major Anand received a hotline call at six in the evening. It was the General Officer Commanding, Northern Zone, calling from Udhampur. He informed Major Anand about the threat of a terror attack at the camp. A platoon of Special Forces was coming over to the camp to assist them with security and cordon.

In five minutes, the whole camp turned into a battle zone. All the soldiers rolled up for action in positions, taking cover behind their respective bunkers. I was moved out of the tent towards an underground bunker near the officers' mess. Captain Sharma took Varun to a different bunker.

I had to crouch inside a steel post with two soldiers taking their positions on either side. The walkie-talkies were blaring. I was confused. As the Special Forces came into the campus, there was a sudden commotion.

'SF is here,' the two soldiers around me murmured. The maroon barrettes were the most decorated soldiers in our country. Their training was the hardest and to get through the same, they had to toil with their blood and sweat. For the mere mortals, it was a fantasy to wear the maroon cap on their heads. As they walked in, the soldiers stood up and saluted the officer.

'Anyone else here with you?' He questioned.

'Sir, a civilian here.' One of the soldiers pointed at me. The officer came forward and offered his hand.

'It's not safe for civilians here,' he said. Both of us headed towards his pickup. His left hand clutched my arm, and his right firmly set around his weapon.

'There are other civilians around here. What about them?'

'We have different groups to evacuate everyone,' he replied confidently. I went along and sat in the vehicle. Four soldiers boarded the vehicle as soon as I sat down. I saw three other vehicles around and wondered if they were picking up Varun as well. A minute later, the engines of two of the cars came to power, and we veered towards the exit. From the corner of my eye to my right, I saw Captain Sharma standing with Varun.

Instantly, I realised that this wasn't an evacuation or any rescue mission. It was important for me to remain calm as I saw Varun signal something. To find the underlying cause, I had to comply with the Special Forces men. The vehicles zigzagged around the corners at high speed. Five minutes into the ride, the officer received a call. From what I heard of the conversation, someone had sent him orders.

He just responded with 'OK' and 'Yes, Sir'. My gut feeling suggested that Mr Bhat or Viktor were about to take over my custody. Anyone apart from these two and I would be in danger. I recollected the line of my father from the audio tape.

Keep on breathing and take a good look at the surroundings.

The vehicle in front of us turned right while our vehicle quickly veered towards the left and came to a halt near a shop. The shutter of the shop opened instantly, and two men approached. Their faces were covered. The tall man on the left seemed like Viktor. He greeted the officer sitting in the front seat and ordered me to come out.

We went inside the shop. The Special Forces vehicle shifted gears and accelerated in the darkness. A lampshade on the extreme right corner was shining bright. Mr Bhat stood there, looking forlorn as I strode towards him.

'How are you? How were the last three days?' he asked without taking his eyes off the lamp.

'Adventurous,' I replied instantly.

'Looks like the young lad is ready to be a man then. You have already learned techniques for saving your life in different circumstances. I hope you haven't discussed me or Viktor with anyone. Although, even if you have, we don't give a rat's fuck.'

'No, I didn't discuss anything. You can cross-check if you want to.'

'We don't need to. They will come to us with their report about you,' he replied, leaving me flabbergasted. The chain of command in the Valley seemed like puzzles combined to give it an impenetrable layer.

'The Special Forces and Rashtriya Rifles units report to you?' I asked. My mind was bustling with curiosity. The secrets of the Valley intrigued me beyond my belief.

'Not really. Sometimes we force them to. After all, it's the government that calls the shots,' he replied, providing a cushion to my curiosity.

'It's time to move,' Viktor said as he approached the two of us. I stood there transfixed, looking at the master spies as Bhat Uncle pushed a button near the lamp. The wall behind it moved a couple of feet towards the left, leading us into an alley. We went down a staircase on the left, hidden by a garbage dumpster.

Taking a right, we headed into a dark passage that allowed only one of us to pass at a time. It was cold as hell. We could hear each other's breath. Mr Bhat asked me to calm down and breathe slowly. We walked for a kilometre in pitch darkness. I didn't have the guts to ask them anything. I felt my heart resigned to the fate these two had decided for me.

I was wondering what was on the other side of this tunnel. It culminated in a shop basement. We went out, and I saw a small complex on the left and some houses on the right.

'Are these your safe passages?' I asked, looking at Bhat Uncle, hoping for an answer. He didn't flinch and kept on walking.

'Keep walking with us, and don't ask questions,' Viktor snapped as he wrapped his right arm around my shoulder.

Safe House

'This was a safe house for the terrorists from the Hizbul cadre. Your father spent at least three months here, warming himself near the fireplace you are standing next to,' Bhat Uncle declared.

He was standing near the wooden ledge overlooking the numerous houses around. All the structures looked quite similar and gave an eerie feeling. I wondered how people identified their houses in this area when even the paint was similar. As soon as he disclosed the startling information, the answer swept right in front of my eyes. Safe houses needed to have camouflage.

'How are you so sure?' I asked, bereft of maturity. He smiled and continued looking outside. After a few seconds, he let out a sigh, took another drag on his brown-coloured pipe and glanced piercingly towards me.

'You should be able to answer this question easily. In case you can't, I will hold Viktor responsible. You haven't been taught well, it seems,' he said.

'I think I know the answer. It was just an immature question originating from my out-of-control curiosity.'

'You need to channel this curiosity. I promise you; it will help immeasurably.'

'Yes, I will try,' I replied and went towards the area I presumed to be the kitchen. I was looking for some water. The fear of death was still troubling me. Despite all this, I was trying to put up a brave front. I had to find my father's truth. As I drank water, for an instant, my mind went to the sign Varun had made while I was being evacuated from the camp.

A similar sign or style was inscribed on the bottle of water. At first, I thought he was signalling me to call him, but I didn't have his number or a working phone. I thought of asking Bhat Uncle about this symbol but refrained. I needed to use my own mind to get a first-hand experience of this world.

I felt I was being too dependent on these two men. The jungle test seemed to be the first of many inconvenient things I might come across in the future.

'Did my father only work with Hizbul?' I asked him.

'Yes, that was the only terrorist organisation active during his tenure.'

'What about JKLF and others?'

'They were the originals, but their ideology was always towards Kashmir freedom. They didn't want to align with our erstwhile neighbour. Basically, they were separatists and have always been.'

'But they killed people. Didn't they? That should make them terrorists if not anything else.'

'Yes, they did. Later, the Indian establishment gave them a long rope to acclimatise with the mainstream. They did a good job. They aren't terrorists anymore.'

'No, they didn't. They have always remained separatists or terrorists. Everything that the media shows happening in the Valley begins and ends with these separatists, and you are saying that they did a good job in getting involved with the mainstream.

'Why have they ordered so many shutdowns in the city for the last thirty years? Why have they given a call for freedom to the youngsters who wanted to study? Why have they always used their monetary power to motivate little children to pick up stones instead of books?' I was flabbergasted by his admission that these separatists were now ordinary citizens and were fully involved with the state subjects.

'I see you have multiple questions. I can answer them one by one, or all at once. How would you like it?'

'One by one. I need to know your point of view.'

'OK. Fair enough. Although you have the freedom to make your own perspective.'

He gave me a detailed perspective about his thoughts on the whole state and its subjects. He was a fan of reformation and always cared for all the terrorists and *Ikhwan* who wanted to enter the mainstream. Because of him, my father could realise his potential and work to the best of his abilities.

Otherwise, my father would have been hunted down and killed by the security forces. He was all in favour of giving and taking equally. He believed that the separatists had a lot to offer to the nation and thus were to be respected. He spoke for a good five minutes or so, but it didn't change my perspective.

My belief was firm, and my thoughts went to Varun's words, 'Mr Bhat is one of the best storytellers Kashmir has ever had.' I told Bhat Uncle about my thoughts. Nothing was going to modify my belief.

Recon with Viktor

Along with the AD of Intelligence, I was asked to conduct a reconnaissance of multiple areas in the Valley. We separated into two teams of four each. Viktor and his guard carried concealed weapons. To mingle with the local population, we wore phirans and spoke Kashmiri.

The other team members spoke more fluently than I did. They had been living in these areas for two years. Additionally, I was also working on a virtual recon. Two of us were making female profiles on social media and dating apps, considering my previous experience in the software field. We had to mingle with random men across the city and find any potential terror sympathisers.

Our teams combed villages along the route from Srinagar to Pahalgam. Viktor informed me about an ongoing threat related to Amarnath Yatra. I argued with him about the government creating fear among the pilgrims amidst the abrogation of Article 370. He told me that no collateral damage was much better than answering a hundred deaths.

'So, the threat this time is real?' I finally mustered the courage and asked him.

'Yes, it is,' he replied with the same poker-faced expression that I had started to associate with him. 'Not only to the pilgrimage route but to the whole of South Kashmir. It's speculated that Sadiq Khan is here.'

'Isn't he the most wanted terrorist in Kashmir? The man who has never been identified or clicked.'

'Yes, absolutely. That's what makes him more dangerous.'

'But South Kashmir is a hotbed for terrorists. Are they going to kill their own people?' I was still confused about many things, and my curiosity did not seem to die down.

'In fact, for a long time, he has been working with us. The latest news is that he has finally found his true purpose and wants to destroy Kashmir. They have no issues with spreading mayhem. Their own or not hardly matters.'

'I disagree on this part. Their fight is against the infidels.'

'This time, they are not only coming for the infidels.'

'Then? Also, how good are your sources?'

'They won't kill. They will destroy the economy. I trust my sources with my life, if not more.'

'How?'

'There will be bombings. Rivers will be destroyed.'

'Destroying a river? Who are we dealing with here? You said terrorists are here, are they scientists as well?' I asked multiple questions and started giggling. I could not digest the fact that religious fundamentalism would one day make infiltrators so competent that they would plan and destroy a river.

'These people are being trained by foreign forces which our neighbour has joined hands with,' Viktor replied quickly.

'Oh, my man Viktor, how many rivers in this world have been destroyed by terrorist acts? Not even one, according to my knowledge. I may not be an intellectual like you and your boss, but I know enough to frame an opinion about what's right and wrong.'

'You seem brainwashed today. Did you meet anyone last night?'

'Yes, my conscience,' I replied and moved ahead.

'The mission is still in progress,' Viktor shouted at me from behind.

'I am progressing towards it. You are the one lagging,' I replied and smiled a bit, looking at the picturesque village ahead. My heart felt content for the first time since I set feet in the Valley. I had finally found my voice and didn't want to let go of it. A few minutes later, I asked him about the details of the intelligence report.

He told me about an absurd plan of small-magnitude blasts at the base of the glacier from which the Lidder River originated. The blasts were planned using a chemical that could mix with the river water and spread everywhere evenly. I tried hard to make sense of this plan but was unable to.

'Are you saying they are trying to poison the river?' I asked him.

'Not exactly, but yes. That's what seems to be the plan.'

'Was a similar plan hatched in 1989, when terrorism was in its nascent stages here?'

'I am not sure.'

'The plan to overflow the rivers of Kashmir was called Operation Lidder.'

'How do you know this?'

'Your boss briefed me about it. My father worked on that operation with him.'

After one week of combing villages along the highways, we finally settled around to check the identified areas in Srinagar. Being the hotspot, Downtown was to be checked the last. It took Viktor three days to complete the Srinagar operation. Ten days of hard work led to the arrest of thirty-two individuals from different areas.

I had no idea if they had anything to do with terrorists, but Viktor seemed confident. On the last day, Viktor gave me an individual task to identify sources we could use for information. I was to stay back in Srinagar city while he was to report to Mr Bhat. He made a few calls and got me a reservation at a hotel opposite Dal Lake.

Was I getting a hang of things? I wondered as we parted ways. Boulevard Road awaited me yet again.

Hotel Paramount

22 August 2019

I was besotted with the magnificence of Dal Lake. The cold evening breeze had started to pick up. Empty houseboats were in the middle of the lake, floating like small objects in a peaceful ocean. The mountains across the lake glittered with the rays of the setting sun. If there was ever a moment to capture with your camera, it was here. I had started to consider myself lucky for deciding to come to Kashmir.

Amidst the clouds of so many thoughts, I completely forgot that I had ordered tea and some Kashmiri bread. A few minutes later, a knock on the door jolted me back to the present.

'Sir, your order.' Rehaan, a member of the hotel staff, spoke from across the door. I had specifically asked the manager to let Rehaan cater to my orders. He was the only one interested in stories about Kashmir and history. For the last three days, we exchanged tales, anecdotes and history about the Valley.

For an eighteen-year-old hotel staff, he seemed far too intelligent. His knowledge was priceless. The versions of different events he narrated were opposite to what I knew. I understood that the information circulated here was always the narrative fed into the minds of the people. I didn't try to counter his point of view rather I listened patiently. As a result, he always gave full attention to whatever I spoke from my limited knowledge.

As I opened the door and collected the tray from him, I felt a strange sensation. I couldn't fathom what exactly it was, but it seemed as if someone was keeping a watch over me. I asked Rehaan to come inside and kept the door slightly ajar. Standing on the left side of the door, I listened with rapt attention for footsteps or any noise.

I signalled him to say something loudly as he looked at me with surprised eyes. He began talking about the weather, which had been surprisingly cold. As soon as he stopped talking, I saw a shadow. Instinctively, I swung the door open and looked towards the staircase.

'Shit,' I whispered. There was no one in the hallway, but I tried to comprehend the possibilities. I asked Rehaan about the number of visitors on this floor. He told me the property owner wouldn't allow an unethical practice like that and asked me to excuse him. He went outside the door and tried to close it. He tried a few times, but the latch did not fall through.

'Sir,' he called out while I was getting ready to light a cigarette on the balcony. Between the latch holder and the wooden door was a black piece of paper. I took it out carefully and observed. My doubts were confirmed. Someone was keeping an eye on me.

The piece of paper was folded in four turns. Unfolding each part increased my heartbeat by a few notches.

'6+33+33+8-6+33-2+8-4+88+555+7777+44+2+66'

This was the message written on the paper with a red sketch pen.

'Is this a fucking joke?' I blurted out, unmindful that Rehaan was still looking at me. He did not respond while continuing to look at me. I looked again at the note and realised that he was still there. I politely asked him to leave me alone. He told me to call him in case I needed anything.

'Will you do me a favour?'

'Sure.'

'Keep your eyes open for anyone who seems suspicious.'

'I will do my best. Will inform you by evening.' Rehaan left soon after, and I headed towards the balcony. The cigarette ash soon filled the table. I was unmindful that the ashtray was not in its original place. My life at that moment felt like that ash, strewn across a table without a starting or ending point.

Anantnag

22 August 2019

'Has Wajahat reported from his position?' Bhat Saab asked Viktor. He was pouring single malt from his favourite bottle while Viktor arranged snacks on the table.

'Yes, he has. The package is fine,' Viktor replied, his eyes fixated on the table.

'Good. Hopefully, he won't turn rogue like his father.' Mr Bhat handed him his glass and sat upright on the brown leather sofa.

'I'm still not sure about his abilities. He tends to believe in stupid things.'

'Does he have too much of this?' Mr Bhat asked and winked while raising his glass. He clinked it with his left index finger.

'I doubt if he would be able to handle even one small of this. It is the finest one could get in this part of the country,' Viktor replied.

'I disagree. There is a better one.'

'Have you kept that hidden?'

'Yes, we shall open that once we see the light of success.'

'Amen,' Viktor said and raised his glass as a toast. Bhat Saab took a sip from his glass and smiled mischievously. He signalled him to get up and come near him. Their eyes met, and Viktor kept his glass on the table while moving towards him. He seductively took Mr Bhat's glass and sipped some whiskey.

'It's time to open something else right now,' Viktor said as he sat on Bhat's lap facing him. His fingers moved towards the side table to switch off the light as he felt the alcoholic breath of Mr Bhat linger on his neck. The man who called himself the saviour of Kashmir for the Indian political system had only one weakness. A rare set of people occupying the topmost chairs were aware of it.

The Recruit

Dinner was about to be served, and I was still staring at the note, trying to comprehend the numbers. Rehaan knocked on the door and ushered in.

'Sorry, Sir, I haven't been able to find anything. It seems a ghost.'

'It's ok, Rehaan, I will try to decode everything myself.'

'I hope you do,' he blurted and went towards the other rooms, leaving the door ajar. I picked up my glass and quickly finished the cheap rum I had been drinking. My head felt light. I went towards the ground floor dining hall when I felt someone staring at me.

'I am feeling spooked all the time,' I said to myself as I continued moving forward. The pair of eyes were still fixated on me, and as soon as I entered the hall, someone called my name from behind. It was another helper running towards me, asking me to halt.

'Sir, someone handed me this card for you.'

'Who?' I asked quickly.

'I don't know. He had come to use the washroom. He was standing right there when he asked me to hand over this to you.' He pointed to the direction of the store, the spot I had passed seconds ahead. The eerie feeling inside me rose by a few notches. Someone was trying to intimidate me in every aspect.

'Where did he go?' I asked while rushing towards the staircase.

'He must have left by now,' he said and started to walk quickly alongside me. Jumping over multiple stairs, we reached the reception area. It was empty.

'Where is the receptionist?' I asked the helper. He ran towards the main door and tried to call the receptionist.

'He must have gone out for a smoke. No one really comes in at this hour.'

'Someone came in and gave this note to you while you claim that no one enters the premises. What will open your eyes?' I shouted and went towards the dining hall. I hadn't noticed the nameplate on the helper's chest. His name was Wajahat. I sat at the first table near the door and looked at the card carefully. Embellished in golden letters was:

'Keep your eyes and ears open. I am looking right at you. Viktor.'

The next fifteen minutes went in a haze. I ordered and ate quickly. I had no idea of the present time; my mind focused on things elsewhere. Rehaan came and asked me about the food a couple of times. I smiled and complimented him as usual. I wanted to find the helper who had given me the card, but he was nowhere around the dining hall.

Rehaan came with the cheque for me to sign. He told me I was looking pale and requested me to rest. I returned to my room, not knowing that another surprise message awaited me. A small yellow envelope was on the tray of the water bottles. I scrutinised it carefully before opening it. It consisted of a bundle of notes. I calculated the amount to be ten thousand and gradually started checking the notes, one by one. On the nineteenth note was the information I was looking for.

'Tomorrow, 10 am.'

The Hotel Room

My heart raced as I went to the balcony and felt the cold air hit my nostrils. I lit a cigarette and inhaled. The stars were shining amidst the blue sky. The Dal Lake looked mesmerising and calmed me a little. I took the five hundred rupees note with the message and neatly folded it into the ashtray.

The cigarette ash didn't burn it completely, so I had to light another match. While at it, I realised that the postcard from Viktor was to be treated the same way. I had heard my father mentioning on the audio tape about destroying all the evidences of communication. I recollected the tip that having an immaculate memory can keep you one step ahead of the enemy.

After composing myself, I decided to listen to the audio recording of my father again. I had started to believe that the tips and tricks in the clip would help in the future.

If I am to learn this trade, why not learn from the best? I thought to myself.

Over the next twenty minutes, I learned that listening and understanding were the best things a man could do.

'Every word spoken on this tape has multiple meanings and can be interpreted in multiple ways.'

Listening to his voice made me all the more emotional.

'To the future, hope you listen to this someday and feel proud that I worked for the betterment of the nation.'

As I heard further, I realised that many points were for the agency professionals, and I wasn't one of them. I learned a few important things, though.

'Keeping your eyes and ears open meant that a person has ordered surveillance on you and has multiple men keeping a tab on your whereabouts.

'Meet me outside meant to check around yourself for followers, and change your location to avoid tracing.'

I paused the tape and contemplated. Viktor got me this hotel room and gave me the task of creating informers. He knew what I was doing and at what time.

Who is helping me? I wondered and played the tape again. I wanted to listen to everything carefully and learn it by heart.

'Any message written or received in numbers is meant to be decoded on an electronic device.' As my father said this on the recording, I heard the sound of a computer keyboard in the background. *Was that number code to be deciphered on a simple mobile phone?* I thought and ran downstairs. I caught hold of Rehaan near the kitchen and asked him for his phone. He took out his smartphone. I needed the smaller one.

As I pressed the required numbers on the keys, I realised Mr Bhat had given me the gold on a platter. After thanking Rehaan, I returned to my room and listened to the audio again. *There were some points that I had to learn by heart*, I thought to myself.

The code was:

'6+33+33+8-6+33-2+8-4+88+555+7777+44+2+66.

M+E+E+T-M+E-A+T-G+U+L+S+H+A+N.'

Gulshan Dhaba

23 August 2019

The next morning, around ten, I was ready to head out. It was a sunny morning, and I informed Rehaan about my plan. I wanted the other helpers to overhear the conversation. I was beginning to use the tricks from the tape.

The area was under a partial lockdown. My curfew pass was carefully placed inside the wallet. I saw a police officer approach in his scooter and asked for a lift. He obliged. I told him I was on official duty and needed to go towards the highway.

He dropped me on the outskirts of Srinagar and asked me to wait for the next convoy or vehicle. I walked some distance and ensured that I wasn't being followed. After waiting for twenty minutes, I hopped onto a minibus going towards South Kashmir.

My destination was 10 Km away, and I was confident

I would be safe. The other passengers on the bus were soldiers and two civilians. As I reached the dhaba, Jahangir recognised me and asked me to sit at the table near the cash counter.

'Like father, like son,' he said softly, audible only to my ears. A CRPF team was having their breakfast. 'This place used to be filled with travellers. God save us from this lockdown,' Jahangir remarked. 'Will you have *Kehwa*?' He asked in a friendly tone.

'Yes, please. And some *Katlam* (a crispy bread baked in a tandoor) as well.'

'Make yourself comfortable. It will take ten minutes,' he said, pointing towards the backpack on my shoulders.

'Oh, I completely forgot,' I said and kept the backpack on the floor near the chair. I took out a book and stretched my legs a little. The fresh breeze coming from the mountains across the highway energised me. I was waiting for the person who had sent the message in the currency to contact me.

I was anxious. Five minutes later, Jahangir emerged from the kitchen with a tray. He got two cups of tea and baked bread. After handing me the cup and saucer, he sat down on the chair opposite me.

'Riyaz always used to like his *Kehwa* in this style. Take a sip and tell me if it's good,' he said.

'It's excellent.' The aroma of saffron filled my nostrils. I smiled.

He lit a smoke and offered me one. 'I know you smoke,' he said.

Was he keeping tabs on me? I wondered.

'Your dedication to this brand has never wavered. Has it?' Inhaling deeply, I asked him.

'Not even for a day,' he replied proudly.

'Do you know why I have been called here?'

'What do you think?'

'Someone wanted to meet me.'

'Absolutely. But who?' he asked.

'I wouldn't have asked you if I knew.'

'You can make an intelligent guess. After all, you are learning from the self-proclaimed best minds of Kashmir,' he said in a sarcastic tone and chuckled.

'You?'

'Your Highness has guessed partially. There is someone else who wanted to meet you as bad as I did,' he said and took out his mobile. He dialled a number and mumbled. 'Come over now. All clear.'

'I have started to get fidgety.'

'You should take a deep breath. You are safe as long as I am alive. Also, I have something for you.'

'Something to do with my father?'

'Yes. An audio recording. Don't worry; it doesn't have tips and tricks. It has something far bigger than anything you know about your dad.'

'Is it?'

'That audio is the only thing that has kept me from going insane all these years. I am still waiting for the completed version, though. As I said, leave all your worries at the door and strive towards the truth,' he said and pointed to the entry. I turned around and saw the mid-noon sun gripping the mountains with its luminescence.

Jahangir went inside the kitchen and came out with a laptop. For the next five minutes, I listened with rapt attention. My father's voice was breaking in certain parts. It seemed that the audio was recorded under extreme circumstances.

A few minutes later, I felt someone move behind me. I turned around and got another shock. It was Varun standing tall and smiling, looking at Jahangir and me. Both of us got up at the same time to wish him. He went towards Jahangir and embraced him.

'Are you going to get me the best *Kehwa* of Kashmir?' Varun asked him and smiled. I was standing perplexed at the bonhomie between the two.

'I will be back in a bit,' Jahangir said and went inside the kitchen.

'You look the same as you did 12 days back,' Varun said, patting my shoulder.

'Were you expecting me to change in such a short period?'

'No, not much. I was just expecting you to look a little less shabby. I thought Bhat's team would let you rest a bit. Have they treated you well?'

'Yes, so far so good.'

'Glad to know that. I understand you have been a part of operations with Viktor. Are you still on some engagement?'

'Yes. Have to make new contacts and informers.'

'I can help you in making a few. Although you will have to do me a favour.'

'What exactly is the favour?'

'You will have to accompany me for a small trek uphill.'

'Any details that I should be aware of beforehand?'

'Nothing as such. Just that your perspective about everything in the Valley might change after that trek.'

'Sounds interesting. When are we going? I would have to plan it. There are people keeping tabs on me, including you.'

'Me? Are you kidding? I am not a spy.'

'How did you contact me then using that message on currency and that paper in the hotel?'

'I didn't. I asked Jahangir to. He is the point man.'

'Everything and everyone here is so mysterious.'

'Absolutely. You will meet multiple people, spies, agents, informers, etc. All of them will proclaim themselves as the best in business. You shouldn't trust anyone.'

'Who exactly is the best in business, then?'

'No one. The best was your father, and now you are here to take back what you were born for.'

'Was I born to be a spy? Don't fool me, Varun.'

'Not any ordinary spy, Raheel. Your father and you are the true saviours of Kashmir.'

'Looks like you read a prophecy somewhere,' I said and laughed. I was starting to wonder if that age-old formula to listen and let go was finally making sense. My maternal uncle always asked me to follow that to remain sane in any circumstance. Everyone was keen to push me up a tree till the only option for me would be to jump or fall.

'Yes, I did. Someone related to you read it to me.'

'Who?' I asked. I was damn curious. At the same time, Jahangir came out with more tea and baked bread.

'I am here, guys,' he shouted.

'You will meet her when we go on the trek,' Varun replied slowly. We discussed multiple things over tea for the next couple of hours. Varun knew more about my father compared to me. He had done a study on almost all the Kashmiris who were, in some way or the other, involved with intelligence agencies.

Jahangir, on the other hand, was the secret keeper of everything Kashmiri. I got to pick their brains and gain enough knowledge. While I was leaving, Jahangir asked me to keep the audio safe. Varun assured that he would get in touch with Jahangir's help.

Hotel Return

I deleted the audio before I returned to the hotel. The assignment was still pending. Four days and no progress meant a beating down from the hard taskmaster, Viktor. I asked for Rehaan's assistance in forging friendships around the hotel. As per Viktor, the Valley was under imminent threat.

Dal, being the most important tourist location, was categorised as a red zone of targets. Rehaan suggested talking to tour guides and travel operators, but none would have spoken to an outsider like me. No one was willing to risk their lives against radical terrorism. They believed that informers and agents were safe only in the villages.

Moreover, they didn't want to receive the tag of being on the payroll of the Indian establishment. Innovation was the need of the hour, and I was looking for ideas. Rehaan told me that people had started looking at him with suspicion, and he wouldn't be able to get work done. One tour operator even asked me to hand over my curfew pass to him. He clicked a picture of my ID.

Rehaan suggested trying some offbeat techniques. The security agencies were on high alert, more so after Article 370 was abrogated. People came out of their homes only to buy essential items.

I needed people who had their eyes and ears open all the time. Rehaan pointed me in the correct direction. In one of the by-lanes, overlooking a two-storied, brick colour house, was a bakery shop. Fondly called *Koshur Kandur*, it translates to 'Kashmiri bakery'. Usually, the bakery people worked for more than 16 hours a day. During the lockdown, they were open for only three hours. Catering in a densely populated neighbourhood meant a lot of hard work.

I had been an erstwhile fan of the bakery and used to relish the bread dipped in ghee as well as the crispy ones with *Kehwa*. The next evening, I strolled out for a walk and returned with a bag full of bread. I distributed most of it amongst the hotel staff with Rehaan's help.

One of the bakery guys seemed friendlier and asked if I was a tourist there. I replied in Kashmiri, startling him for a second. After composing himself, he welcomed me and told me about the prevailing situation. The bakery became a regular spot for me. I indulged in discussions with them and even discussed opening a tea shop near theirs.

They advised me against it, for the local Muslims wouldn't like it. An outsider settling and establishing a business in that area was a strict no. Three days after discussing politics, Kashmir, India and other topics, I tried my luck at flushing information about anti-social elements. Asking them directly about potential or existing terror threats in the area would have invoked suspicion.

I discussed the arrest of youngsters during the crackdown after 5 August. One of them started warming up to me, and I invited him over for a drink at the hotel that evening. Three glasses of Old Monk finally did wonders. He gave me the names of four people living in the colony adjacent to his.

All of them were active terrorists or over-ground workers with sympathy for the terrorists. I laughed it off in front of him. The banter continued similarly for the next three nights. On one of those nights, I walked him back to his place. I had to understand the demographics to provide valuable input to Viktor.

After ten days of staying at Hotel Paramount, I made enough progress to inform Viktor. The only thought plaguing me was that I had no idea how to reach him. It had been a week since I met Jahangir and Varun. I wondered if they would reach out to me. My patience had started running thin.

Breakfast

30 August 2019

The next morning, as I went down for breakfast, a shocker was lying in wait. For the last few days, with Rehaan's assistance, I was sitting at the same table every day. From the door, I saw a man already sitting at that table. Burly in frame, wearing a hoodie. Instinctively, I started moving towards the other table on the right but stopped. I was five feet away when he spoke in that familiar heavy voice.

'You are four minutes earlier than your usual breakfast time,' Viktor announced himself back on the scene. He even knew my breakfast timing, and it bothered me.

'How have you been?' I asked him.

'Better than you. Although, I missed your presence during the last weeks' operations.'

'Good to know.'

'Have you made any progress?' He asked, coming straight to the point.

'I suggest we eat first,' I replied and signalled Rehaan to get plates and tea. I ate quickly, having drunk too much the previous night, while Viktor went on slowly. He chewed the bread and omelette carefully, sipping tea every time to wash it down. His eyes were piercing my hidden thoughts.

After finishing the food, I told him the detailed results of my task. I told him about the over-ground workers in the locality of the bakery and the necessity of profiling them.

'We need to do a closer check of that area. Probably, you should get more comfortable with your bakery friends.'

'I am already on good terms with them.'

'Make the terms work for you then.'

'I will try my best. Don't worry.'

'No, I am not worried. The nation is.'

'When Raheel is here, the nation shouldn't fear.'

He started laughing and said, 'I hope you don't go crazy. Kashmir doesn't have a good record in letting people maintain sanity.'

'I will try,' I replied, embarrassed.

'By the way, you should learn how to cover your tracks. Do you know why Jahangir's tea stall is called Gulshan Dhaba?' He asked all of a sudden. My face turned pale. It felt as if the blood flow in my upper body had stopped, leaving me numb. My throat started drying up, and my right hand on my thigh involuntarily curled into a punch.

Thoughts started crossing my mind, but I tried not to give anything away to him. My anger was getting the better of me. How would I forgive myself if anything happened to Jahangir because of my foolishness?

'I don't know. I only went there once with Bhat uncle,' I lied with a straight face, looking right into his eyes. He smirked. A second later, I realised that he had seen through me. Lying to your mother about a party and lying to a spy about an informer were entirely different things. That day, I learned I still had a long way to go in this business.

'Well, let me tell you. Gulshan was Jahangir's son. He lost his life in the unrest in Kashmir after the hanging of Maqbool Bhat in 1984. The boss asked me to tell you this. He also specifically mentioned that Jahangir treats you as his son, and his sons do not usually have a long life. It would be better not to engage in any personal business with that man.'

'Are you threatening me?' I asked in a tone firm enough to make him realise that I wasn't going to take this shit.

'No, I am letting you know the thoughts of the man you work for.'

'I work for myself. No one else.' I raised my voice even further. My right peripheral vision was repeatedly pointing me to the helper standing three tables on my right. He had been cleaning the table for the last ten minutes and keeping an eye on us.

'Keep reminding yourself the same thing. It might

help you to remain sane,' Viktor replied, totally composed. An hour later, I was lying on the hotel bed, contemplating Viktor and my actions over the last ten days.

Somehow, it hit me. I had missed an individual in the minibus who was wearing a brown colour headgear. I tried to recollect how his eyes looked but couldn't. I realised he had only seen me enter the dhaba and didn't know anything about Varun or what we discussed.

I expected an increase in the surveillance. Meeting Varun or expecting him to contact me in such circumstances seemed inappropriate. There was only one way to reach out to Jahangir–one of the bakery people had to go for a ride. I spent the whole day planning how.

Encounter with Raja

The evening sky was overcast. A strong breeze was blowing from the west. The door to the balcony, which I had kept open all these days, suddenly started shaking due to the wind. I managed to drag my tired body out of the bed to shut the door. As soon as I stepped into the balcony, it started raining.

My mind raced towards the cigarette box and matchsticks on the chair outside. I picked them up and tried to remove traces of water from them. The pack of cigarettes was the second most important company I had kept over the last three weeks in the Valley.

The most important was of course the memories of my father and the will to know more about him. I wished that the rain had given way to snowfall. I had never seen snow in my life. During my college, many asked me if I had seen snowfall. Having denied umpteen times made me realise that Kashmir was something I had been missing since birth.

A chilly gush of wind hit my spine as I bent down to fix the latch on the door. After returning to the safe havens of my blanket, I decided to prioritise living in Kashmir for at least a few months every year. I knew convincing my mother would be tough, but then nothing was impossible.

I decided to read the remaining write-ups given by Mr Bhat. The title on the left top of the page in tattered handwriting read *The Unforgivable Tragedy*. When Bhat Uncle had given me the audio recording and other pages, I deliberately decided not to read this particular write-up. The first line itself sent waves of agony across my soul.

Crying for your loss is not so easy, but when you kill a friend with your own hands to keep your agenda ticking, something dies inside you. Everything died for me during that fierce encounter with a party of J and K police near village Tehgram in Kupwara.

Tilak Kumar led the party. 'Raja', as he was fondly called, was the son of a village sarpanch. He had the aura of a king. He was magnanimous but displayed an authoritative attitude when it mattered the most. Getting work done was his forte. I met him for the first time when Mr Bhat had sent a few of his associates to bail me out from the local police station in Anantnag. It was 1988.

He entered the police station with such charisma that even the SHO stood up in attention. At that time, he had links with the jail authorities in Jammu and Kashmir. His contacts were so influential that he could get a man freed out of Tihar Jail. While having tea at a roadside stall near the police station, I was drawn to his humour.

Being almost the same age, he took a keen interest in my past and present. He empathised with me and suggested joining the police or any other security agency. Being strictly against vengeance, he warned me about the consequences.

Years later, on that fateful night, while I was bringing some men across the border into Kupwara, Tilak was leading a team of counter-insurgents. My face was covered. Such was his firebrand nature that he didn't even wear a bulletproof jacket in the encounter while others had full protective gear on them.

I remember his first bullet grazing my shoulder as I was leading the terrorists. Immediately after taking cover, I asked my men to lie low for a minute so that I could verify who was firing upon us. He didn't even crouch or take cover. He was standing upright behind a thick tree trunk with his rifle pointed straight at me.

I could sense palpable tension around me. These police officers were jeopardising my mission, and I couldn't talk them out of this situation. Bullets were striking the trees inches above where our heads were. I asked the men I was leading to scatter in two opposite directions while I stayed put. I started firing from different positions, taking effective cover of the thick forest and the moonless night.

The men rolled over on their bellies and started firing on the police from two different positions. I tried to stay focused amidst the barrage of bullets when a shrieking voice echoed among the trees. One of the terrorists had his face blown off by a bullet from the police team. I was starting to lose patience.

Taking their leader out was the only option. I didn't want the blood of any patriot on my sleeves, but this had to be done. I unpinned a grenade and threw it towards the tree covering Tilak. He ducked immediately, and his team jumped away to cover themselves from the splinters. I got up and ran towards a boulder on the right. I felt two bullets shot in my direction, but luckily, they were off target.

I was within ten feet of Tilak's position. One mistake and I would have been dead. The boulder and my stance became a hassle for the group of terrorists on the right. I signalled to them with my hands to stop firing, and they obliged. I shouted at Tilak using his pet name, asking him to get out. 'Raja Ji, gasu daffa.'

Startled, Tilak ordered his team to stop firing. He shouted from behind the tree covering him, and his voice echoed–'Che kusu chuk dalla?' (Who are you, pimp?)

'Bastard, I am the God of Death you had embraced long back outside a police station. Get the fuck out of here lest I blow your face,' I shouted back.

'Get your filthy body out of the cover of that boulder, and I shall show you whose gun has more potent gunpowder,' he thundered. The exchange of words somehow worked in my favour as the police officers lost their attention and got hit by precise bullets from the terrorists on the left.

Two of them died on the spot, while three were grievously injured. Tilak was hit in the shoulder, and he fell. I slowly crawled towards him and saw him lying in a pool of blood. Tears filled my eyes as I picked up my Automatic and shot him from a distance of three feet. His body shivered and went cold.

A second later, behind the boulder, I let out a hoarse cry that resonated in the forest. My heart was racing, and my eyes were blood red. I was distraught with what I had done. Tilak was not only a friend, instead his family was like my own. How would I ever face his parents? I thought to myself.

A few minutes later, I went towards the team of terrorists on my right. I asked them to communicate with the others and fixed a vantage point outside the forest. That night, I achieved my objective of helping five armed terrorists infiltrate the Kashmir valley. Exactly fifteen days later, a team of CRPF and BSF killed them while they were hiding in a house in Kupwara. That day, without pulling a trigger, I avenged Tilak's death.

If you ever read this, son, remember that there might come a day when you will have to trample upon your friends and love to fight for what you believe is right. My only piece of advice is–keep your conscience clear.

Ironclad Message

Around six in the evening, Rehaan got two cups of *Kehwa* with some baked bread from the neighbourhood bakery shop. The aroma of tea, mixed with saffron, filled my heart with nostalgia. I was missing my mother. As I applied butter over the bread, I felt something hard on the sides.

A sip of *Kehwa* with the sight of the mighty Dal was beginning to grip my life. I was procrastinating about what I would be doing if I had my own house in the hills. I was about to finish the first bread when a morsel got stuck between my teeth. I thought it to be a small stone in the dough.

I used my tongue to flush it out of my mouth, and it fell on the plate with a thud. It was silver-greyish and shining. I stopped chewing and observed it. Something didn't seem right. I picked it up and realised it was a round toy bullet-shaped piece of metal. Was it sent deliberately to me?

I questioned myself for a second and began to look at it from different angles. Placing the metal on the table, I started inspecting it. It was shining from all angles except one. I used a pen to puncture it. After grappling with it for more than five minutes, I could crack it. The metal split open, and a neatly folded piece of paper emerged.

Bluish-white paper. Black ink. Some numbers and a three-word message. 'Remember the digits'.

A moment later, I was rummaging through my bag, searching for the map of Kashmir with latitude and longitude. The tea started to go cold. The breeze was picking up speed, like my brain. Any experienced intelligence operative would have identified the coordinates in minutes. It took me an hour to decipher the same.

The message was clearly sent by Jahangir but there was no mention of the date and time. At least, I thought so. I looked again and was surprised. The location seemed like a market in Tral village. I had to get ready. The next day was going to usher in a new dawn in my life. While retiring to my room after dinner, I asked Rehaan to get me tea early in the morning.

'Are you planning to go out tomorrow?' He asked.

'Yes, have some work to complete in the nearby areas.'

'Great. Your tea will be ready,' he replied and walked away towards the kitchen. At the same moment, I felt someone keeping a close watch over what I was saying. As I walked towards my room, I felt my senses speaking to me. I realised that someone from the hotel had followed me the last time I went to meet Jahangir.

The same person was there in the hotel, monitoring every move of mine. The same big brown eyes that I saw sitting five rows behind me on the bus. I quickly changed my course and headed towards the exit. Taking a few fast paces, I went outside the hotel towards the left on the street.

This portion of the road was completely out of sight from the kitchen window. I waited, tilting my eyes towards the door. *Would anyone come out to follow me*,I wondered as the next fifteen seconds felt like hours. As soon as my attention started to waver, I heard footsteps approaching.

It was Wajahat. The helper for the first-floor rooms. The same big brown eyes were looking directly at me as I took a step towards the road and lit a smoke. The next morning, I took three detours to ward off the man. I got into a private vehicle heading towards South Kashmir. Fun was about to begin.

Zeba Ji

31 August 2019

On top of a hill, after trekking for around an hour, we finally spotted a house. The path was arduous, and the forest dense. A stream was flowing parallel to our path on the left. The splash of water dwarfed the noise our steps made on the dry leaves around. There was a nip in the air, but we felt quite comfortable with light jackets.

As we stepped into the compound of the house, I heaved a sigh of relief. The main gate was open, and we saw ourselves in. Varun called out but did not receive a response. We went around the left of the house and saw a reflection at the opposite end inside a room. I opened the heavy door, and it creaked.

There were books stacked in piles of twenty-thirty everywhere. As we crossed the kitchen, I caught a familiar aroma. Freshly prepared green lentils, red lotus stem, and steaming hot rice were ready and served on two big plates. I halted for a second, and Varun followed suit. As we stood mesmerised, looking at the two plates full of food, an old woman, holding a brown wooden stick, walked out of a room opposite the kitchen.

'I was expecting both of you,' she said. Her voice was commanding, and her eyes exuded charm. Varun smiled, looking at her while I was confused, still wondering how she knew the time we would reach. Varun quickly went towards her, and they embraced.

'Do you feel shy from your grandmother's sister?' she asked, breaking my thoughts and turning me into a nervous wreck. I looked at both of them alternatively for a few seconds until Varun spoke up.

'I told you. She will be the most important person you will meet in the Valley. Your moment of truth is finally here. Come, embrace it with open arms.'

A shiver went across my spine yet again. I didn't know anyone from my grandmother's family. Meeting Bhat Uncle had given a new dimension to my life, and here I was, adding another facet to it. I gave her a quick hug. Behind the old woman was a portrait. Two adult women hugging an adolescent lovingly. I stared at it for a few seconds when she spoke up.

'He is the one who has been teaching you since you landed in the Valley. My younger brother, he calls himself the saviour of Kashmir but–'

'But?' I asked.

'He has destroyed it beyond measure. Kashmir has slipped out of our hands.'

'Do you mean the hands of the Indian government?'

'No, my boy. The hands of common Kashmiri people. People who want peace and prosperity.'

'Can this situation be reversed?'

'Yes. But for that, we need you,' Varun cut in.

'How?' I was intrigued beyond measure. Kashmir surprised me every day.

'You will have to kill some people,' she said, leaving me shocked. She was smiling as if reassuring me that everything was all right.

'Who are you? What's your name?' I asked without thinking. Both of them started to smile.

'My name is Zeba. I am your grandmother's younger sister.'

'Are you an agent as well?' I asked her like a curious child switching on the bulbs in the house and watching them with intrigue. She started laughing. If Bhat Uncle was intimidating, this woman was giving me chills.

'Agent?' She let out a sigh and repeated the words the way I had said.

'My younger brother must have told you about the intelligence here. He must have proclaimed himself to be the go-to man for Indian policymakers.'

'Yes, he did.'

'He is a consultant. I am sure you are aware of that word. Now, use that for a nation's security, and you will know what he is. On the other hand, I am one of the informal advisors to the National Security Committee. My brother is aware of my position, and that's the reason he hasn't visited me for years. Our family has given their blood for India. Yet, I live here alone in this rotten house while that man enjoys all the facilities of the state in a sponsored bungalow.'

'That didn't look like a sponsored bungalow to me, but it's fine, you are bound to have your opinion. Actually, I face a tricky situation here. I don't know whom to believe, let alone what.'

'It's Kashmir. You don't believe anyone here. Everyone is selfish and opportunistic. Watch every step, and keep looking over your shoulder.'

'Always,' I replied nonchalantly.

'Who would you rather believe? A cunning consultant who lives on State money and spends his nights with his junior men or a woman, living alone in a shitty house on this faraway hill. You came here to find your truth. She will help you with it,' Varun interjected.

'But after a certain point, it will be you alone. In a dark tunnel of lies, finding the brightest spark you will proclaim as the truth of your life,' Zeba Ji cut in, leaving me spellbound.

I looked at both of them and closed my eyes for a second. What if both of them were lying? What if everyone was lying and pushing me into a vicious hole from where I would never return? Was Bhat Uncle really the cunning man they were accusing him of being? Was he really sleeping with his juniors? Was Viktor a part of all this shit happening around me? I had multiple questions. Seeing me lost in thoughts, Zeba Ji went towards the door on her left.

'Koori, come out, it's time. He needs you now more than ever,' she called out. The door opened, and I almost fell off my feet. I held on to a chair for support.

'What on earth are you doing here?' I asked instinctively.

'My duty,' she replied and smiled. As she approached, I started to lose my mind. She came and gave me a warm hug.

'Mum, you shouldn't be here. This place is not safe at all,' I said in a measured tone. She smiled again. A moment later, I looked around and saw all of them with similar expressions. Their smile mocked me. I realised my mistake.

'I have spent my childhood here. It's totally safe when your heart is at peace,' she replied. Zeba Ji came towards me and asked me to take a seat. She patted my shoulder.

'You have already started feeling old,' she said and smiled.

'No, I think the Valley is giving me new lungs,' I replied.

'Maybe you should take deeper breaths and sit upright,' Mum said and gave a mischievous smile.

'Can someone help me understand what is happening?' I sighed.

'You are coming of age, and all of us are helping you cross the boundaries you have set yourself,' Zeba Ji said. I sat there silently, replaying her lines in my mind, 'crossing the boundaries that I had set'. Her words enchanted me.

When my mother called Zeba Ji to inform my visit

to Kashmir and my interest in meeting Mr Bhat, she understood something was wrong. Varun, being the only journalist Zeba Ji trusted, was to keep me under observation. They worked with Jahangir to get messages across to me. Mother, on the other hand, had arrived in Kashmir two days back at the behest of Zeba Ji. Things were about to get interesting.

The Incomplete Truth

'Did he give you an audio recording with Riyaz spelling out instructions?' Zeba Ji asked, bringing me out of the self-questioning stupor.

'Yes, I have that on my phone as well,' I replied. She told me that she had an audio recording, and I should copy its contents as well. I was ready for it.

'Listen to it, but only when you return to your hotel. You might get to know what is happening around you. Also, you will get to do some research as well,' she said.

'But who will answer my questions, if I have any?'

'Son, you will have many questions and you will need to find some of the answers yourself. Neither your mother nor I will be able to come to your rescue. It's your fight, and you need to win it alone. If you want help, Varun will be there with you.'

'Do you mean whatever Bhat Uncle has told me was a lie?'

'No. That doesn't mean he hasn't twisted facts and statements. He is an expert at that. After all, he wants to win at all costs.'

'Yet he proclaims to be a servant of India.'

'He serves the people who are in power, his masters. They don't like losing.'

'I am not sure if I am bothered about his masters, his pay grade, or anything. I'm here to know the truth about my father's life.'

'Well, to get there, you will need to face the arch-enemy of your father.'

'Who's that?'

'The Indian political system.'

'You mean my childhood remained bereft of my dad because of politics?'

'Yes, precisely.'

'How do you suggest I fight the system, that too, from here?'

'You take out their jewel crown. It's as simple as that.'

'What do you mean?'

'You hit them where they get hurt the most. You destroy everything the system holds dear.'

'Easier said than done. What happens to her?' I asked, pointing at my mother, who was stirring the pot inside the kitchen.

'Don't worry about her. She will be here with me.'

'And she won't need me? What if they come for her?'

'They will come for all of us. Be assured of that.'

'Yet, you are asking me to take this plunge.'

'Of course. There is no one apart from you who can destroy the system from within.'

'Are you looking for revenge, Zeba Ji?' I asked her.

'No, she isn't. I am,' Mother announced, having tiptoed towards the sofa from the kitchen. Her eyes were red. Her breath was heavy. Her face expressed indomitable rage. If there was an act of revenge that I wanted to be part of, this was it.

A Disappeared Tourist

That evening, an SOS message was sent to Viktor from a mobile in the Paramount Hotel describing my disappearance. An instant trace came up for my phone. The location displayed the Paramount Hotel, Dal Lake. The software engineer from New Delhi had given a slip to the AD of Intelligence and his team.

Five minutes later, Zeba Ji received a call from Bhat Uncle. After the initial pleasantries, he asked her the question that all of us sitting in the room expected.

'Riyaz's son has gone missing from around Dal Lake. Can you help us find him?'

'God help us from this misery! Did you cause him any trouble?' Zeba Ji questioned back.

'No, I was just helping him in touring a few places around Kashmir. He wants to know more about Riyaz.'

'Ok. Hope you have told him everything.'

'Not everything. I have to tell him a lot more. Help me find him, please.'

'Sure, I will. If I get to know anything about him, you will be the first person to know.'

'Great. Have a good evening.' She kept the phone on the side table and got up. After drawing all the curtains of the house, she returned to her seat and calmly picked up her tea. Sometime later, she got up and started checking outside from the kitchen window.

'Varun Ji, can you go to the terrace to check for intruders around the area?'

'Sure, Zeba Ji. Can I get the binoculars or any night vision?'

'Yes, they are in the box attached to the sofa, right beneath you.' Varun signalled me to accompany him. We checked the perimeter but found nothing.

'Are there chances that people followed us?' I asked Varun.

'You are the super spy. You tell me.'

'I doubt. I feel Bhat Uncle called Zeba Ji out of desperation. His men cannot find me. He must have received a message some time back before he made that call.'

'And why do you think he called Zeba Ji?'

'Because he knows this is the only place I can be. Also, he will be able to confirm mum's travel details by tomorrow and in the next twenty-four hours, he will know that I came here with you.'

'Riyaz Ji must be smiling from the heavens today.'

As soon as we got down, we saw Zeba Ji pulling an old silver trunk out of her bedroom. We offered assistance. She told us she could manage and asked us to take whatever we wanted. Varun opened the trunk lock, and a shockwave engulfed my body. AK-47s, automatic revolvers, country pistols and hundreds of bullets. Zeba Ji had been preparing for war, and we were her foot soldiers.

'Zubeida, please get the food. These gentlemen don't have much time.' Mum came out without food but with an empty rucksack.

'They need this more than food,' she said, smiled and went back in. She was preparing dinner.

'Prepare yourself for revenge,' Zeba Ji said and gave her blessings. I carefully packed an army knife, five magazines and two revolvers.

'Is that it?' Varun asked.

'Yes, that's all I need.'

Finding Light In the Dark

The trek downhill was not arduous. Varun was a great accomplice. Using trees as shields, we made our way towards the Tral market. We didn't need any flashlights. The moon was resplendent. Moreover, Varun was a terrain expert. I asked him about his experience with the routes.

He surprised me by revealing about five different routes to the market. While on our way downhill, the echo of a shrieking sound startled me more than once. He asked me not to pay any heed to the rumbling. A vehicle was already waiting for us near a meat shop. The road behind the market was deserted as we made a quick exit from the forest towards the white Alto.

'I hope you are carrying your pass,' Varun said. I quickly scanned my pockets for the paper that had allowed me to roam around the city without the paramilitary asking questions. He moved towards the rear wheels and found the keys.

'Yes,' I replied.

'Great. Make sure you don't overdo the speed,' he said and threw the keys towards me.

'Am I driving?' I asked.

'Absolutely. I am a journalist. They will have fewer questions for you as compared to me.' We zoomed across the roads in South Kashmir. Boulevard Road was an hour away. We were stopped a few kilometres ahead by the first paramilitary picket. I quickly handed over my pass and got the go-ahead.

'You remember the plan, don't you?' Varun asked.

'Yes,' I replied. With every curve on the road, I took deeper breaths. My body felt pangs of nervousness.

'Do you feel something being on these roads?'

'What do you mean, Varun?'

'Don't you feel closer to your father?

'Closer? Not sure. However, I feel awkward. I feel a sense of belonging. Ever since I saw the majestic Dal, my deepest fears and the best dreams seem to have found a safe place.'

'Interesting. Just how I was expecting an author to say.'

'Don't embarrass me.'

'I'm not. I am only helping you stay attentive. Your legs have been shaking since we left,' he pointed and smiled. We crossed two more checkpoints, and I repeated the same pass. An officer randomly inquired about my boss. I told him an imaginary name, and he stared at me for a moment. He probably knew that such a name didn't exist.

They let us go, and I saw him click the number plate of our car with his phone. We were about to be put under surveillance. Varun asked me to take a shortcut and drive faster. In about ten minutes, we were at the start of Boulevard Road.

'Take this left here,' he said, pointing to a lane ahead of us. I dropped Varun at Hotel Sangram and parked the car outside a hotel a hundred meters ahead on the opposite side of the road. Neither of us spotted a black motorbike parked opposite Hotel Sangram. The bike had followed us from the entry of Srinagar.

My hotel was half a kilometre away. I planned to walk the stretch. Varun told me it was a big risk. He took the rucksack and asked me to wait for his message. He specifically instructed me not to venture out of the hotel room. I nodded in agreement.

I had finally started to behave like my father. I had two handlers on opposite ends of the spectrum. I was following their advice but acting on my instincts. Was this the homecoming I dreamed of years ago?

The Long Walk

I had an eerie feeling. A pair of eyes were piercing me each moment. I looked around but found no one. The hotel stood a hundred meters ahead. Two men outside the entrance were smoking. I stopped in my tracks. Wajahat and Viktor were talking to each other. They looked worried. I took a deep breath as I approached them. I had to look and sound confident. Every action from here was going to be scrutinised.

My mother's words filled my ears–'Everyone told you a story. It's time you conjure one of your own.'

'What a pleasant surprise, Viktor!' I exclaimed as I stepped into the hotel compound. In the next four steps, my mind created an entire sequence of events for the day. I looked at Wajahat with narrowed eyes. 'Aren't you the helper for the first floor here?' He looked at Viktor but did not respond. Viktor signalled him to leave us alone and asked me to accompany him to a bench in the hotel lobby.

'I have something important for you,' he said without looking at me. We walked slowly. I looked around to sense any danger lurking. It felt safe.

'I don't want to know anything about your whereabouts today. I just want to inform you that there is an imminent threat to all of us. The whole team. Your name is in the top three of the list. We have specific input about a blast or an attack around this area tomorrow at noon. Your pictures and name have been leaked. Be careful.'

'Thanks for keeping me in the loop. I will take care. You also be extra careful. I feel your name must figure at the top of that list.'

'You have become smart. Did you meet anyone special?'

'The ghost of my father,' I replied and got up from the bench. I started moving towards the staircase to go to my room. I had crossed half the stairs when a commotion started near the entrance. An explosion and a hail of automatic gunfire. I ran up the stairs and ducked behind the pillar near the first room on my right.

From the gaps in the railing, I saw three masked men enter the hotel. Viktor was lying in a pool of blood, probably still alive. For five seconds, the men resorted to indiscriminate firing all around the hotel. Everyone was startled. People started shouting inside their rooms. The receptionist was hit on the head. I shrieked at the sight but did not move an inch.

I had been looking to emulate my father, and here

I was, afraid and lifeless, ducked behind a pillar for the sake of my life. I felt weak at that moment. I wanted to rush downstairs and help Viktor. I heard a faint noise of a motorcycle starting outside the compound. People started gathering from the nearby hotels.

The terrorists disappeared in a flash. The kitchen staff moved towards the lobby while I sat transfixed at the sight of my college friend. His head and left arm were hanging while he had slumped in the chair. His eyes were fixated on the stairs. My tryst with Kashmir had well and truly started.

I took deep breaths and gathered myself. I decided to go to my room, collect my things, and head to Varun's hotel. As soon as I turned, I saw a familiar shadow through the corner of my left eye. The shining white coat of the helper, the big brown eyes. For the first time in my life, I saw a gun pointed at me from such a close range. I stood right there, not even moving my eyes. Looking straight at the staircase, my mind was instructing me to make a dash for it.

'Was it you who created this mess downstairs?' I asked, trying to unnerve him.

'I am just a pawn,' he shot back with a cunning smile. I tilted my head a little towards him. I wanted to face him head-on. He signalled me to move towards my room.

'Who do you work for?' I asked, knowing well that too many inquisitions could be dangerous for my well-being.

'For Kashmir. For Sadiq Khan. Now shut up and move. Get into your room. I have been instructed not to harm you. They say you are the golden goose,' he said and laughed.

'But you worked for Viktor all this while?'

'This is Kashmir. You don't work for the highest bidder but for the one who sets your soul free,' he muttered.

Why would Sadiq Khan, the most wanted terrorist, plan to protect me? I wondered but didn't dare ask him. The gun was still against my back as we moved along.

Midnight Mayhem

After we left Zeba Ji's place, two men took positions in the nearby orchards. A sniper and a spotter. The curtains of Zeba Ji's house were still drawn. She was about to go to bed when Mother came into her room and complained about the unsettling quietness outside. Zeba Ji got up and started inspecting the surroundings. A few minutes later, she observed something shining outside the attic window.

'Zubeida, switch off all the lights,' she told Mother and went into her room. She bent down to fetch the heavy trunk from beneath her bed. 'Ouch,' she gasped as her knees made a clasping sound. Her arthritis had always been a pain. She took out an old scope and sat near the bedroom window. Mother was uneasy and panting, while Zeba Ji was calm. She scanned the whole area.

'There is no one this side,' she remarked and casually got up. She asked Mother to use the scope and check from the kitchen while she dug deeper inside the trunk and fetched a huge brown-coloured bag.

'Keep away from the windows,' she called out to my mother. They scanned around the kitchen but found nothing. They alternated to keep a watch from the attic window for the next two hours. They were growing suspicious but weren't able to pinpoint the source of their anguish till one of the two men outside got up to take a leak behind a nearby tree.

Zeba Ji saw the man with the rifle signal the other to move a little away. She nodded while looking at Zubeida and asked her to keep vigil. It was going to be a long night.

'Does the national level shooter still have it in her?' Zeba Ji asked. Zubeida smirked.

At about the same time as the attack at our hotel, there were two simultaneous incidents. A grenade was lobbed into the lobby of the Hotel Sangram. Fortunately, no one was injured. Varun was already inside his room. He didn't even dare to come near the window. He knew his life, and everyone else's was in danger.

The whole city was about to explode, and he was going to be a part of it. The entire area started buzzing with security forces. The only occupants of the hotel rooms were paramilitary forces or journalists. Most of them started moving around, inquiring about the incidents. A unit from the RR came to comb the area.

Security forces started using loudspeakers to disperse anyone standing on the road. Small groups of police officers started spreading all over Srinagar.

In Tral, at Zeba Ji's place, two rounds of .338 Magnum were fired from the Scorpio TGT rifle. The first made a dent in the attic window and struck the neck of the sniper outside. The other, half a second later, slammed into the skull of the spotter. The night of eerie silence was jolted apart.

Birds started making noise. The gushing winds were more powerful and tried to force their way inside through the attic window. Kashmir had been given a call to awaken at midnight. Hell was about to be unleashed.

The Mad Man

I entered my room with Wajahat's gun still poking my back. He got a call and, for a moment, fumbled with the gun to reach his mobile in his trouser pocket. I sensed it somehow. As soon as he got the phone out, I turned a bit and poked my right heel into his knee. The gun and mobile both fell out of his hand. He tumbled.

I smashed his ribs with my feet a few times. He still got up, this time ready for a fistfight. A couple of right hooks landed on his jaw, while he came close to knocking me out twice. His right jab was so fearsome and quick that I tried to duck under everything. He was well-built but so nimble that, for a moment, I started regretting not going through physical endurance training.

One of his kicks caught me by surprise. I was hit in the ribs, just below the heart. I fell on my knees. Blood was rushing out of my mouth. He moved towards his revolver, and in that instant, I saw his mobile lying right next to where I was. He bent down, and I sprang up on my feet. I ran across and banged the mobile on the back of his head.

Dizziness took over him as I tried grabbing his gun. I kicked his shin and balls, but he didn't give in. He smashed a gruesome uppercut that hit my nose and left me bloodied. I was done and staring at certain death as he pointed his gun towards me. I closed both my eyes and prayed.

A flash went through my body as a burst of fire almost left me deaf. However, it did not come from Wajahat. He was lying face down at my feet, his skull cracked open. My hands were covered with blood. A man wielding an automatic rifle was standing at the door, covering the entire frame. Captain Sharma, from the RR unit, had come to my rescue. I got up slowly, and he asked me to head towards the staircase.

'My stuff. It's here. I need it,' I murmured.

'My men will get it. Don't worry. Keep on walking. Let's get you out of here,' he replied quickly, taking fast strides towards the exit. Army trucks and police vehicles had cordoned off the area. He asked two of his men to help me into a truck. They asked me to lie on a bench at the far end of the truck.

The scratches were minor, but my head and neck were hurting. My ears were still in shock. As the doctor administered first aid on my battered face, I sensed someone looking at me. Varun was standing right ahead. He was smiling.

'Did you get these guys here?' I asked him slowly. He didn't reply instead came forward and held my hand.

'Yes, I did. There is nothing more important than you in the Valley right now,' he said and smiled, looking right through me. I felt our bond strengthen, and my pain started to decrease. My face had swelling, and my eyes were moist. I tried to get up from the bench, but my back started to ache. He supported me with his arm and helped me sit.

'It's going to be a long night, Writer Saab. Brace yourselves.'

'If you are on my side, I might face a thunderstorm as well.'

'You should not trust a journalist with your life this much.'

'I can trust a man, irrespective of his profession. I learned to comprehend a man's hidden emotions long back. I need not worry about you.'

'Of course, you have a bigger fish to worry about.'

'Fish? He's a crocodile,' I smirked. Five minutes later, the crocodile received a phone call from Zeba Ji. She told Mr Bhat that an army unit had picked up Raheel from a hotel. She asked him to ensure the well-being of her sister's grandson. A cell phone, unattended near the reception of Hotel Paramount kept buzzing for the next ten minutes. The news of Viktor's demise reverberated across Kashmir.

Mr Bhat was pacing up and down his drawing room. His satellite phone and mobile were in his hands. He was making calls at a frantic pace. New Delhi, Punjab, contacts were being questioned everywhere. He was trying to come to terms with Viktor's loss. Who should be held responsible? He questioned himself. His judgement was clouded. The only man he thought could be so extravagant at this time was–Sadiq.

Feeling a little worked up, he went near his bar table. He made a large peg of his favourite single malt, the one he had relished alongside Viktor a few days back. After taking a sip and feeling its aroma, he sank deeper into the sofa. He felt Viktor's smile brightening the room. The moonlit sky was too bad for his comfort.

He wanted to dig a hole of darkness and hide inside. He gulped the glass of whiskey in one go, got up and went slowly into his room. The sadness engulfed his senses as he broke down, crying for the first time after twenty-eight years. That night, Mr Bhat lost the second man he ever loved.

Army Cantonment

Around three in the morning, we reached the nearby cantonment. Varun and I were provided a room to rest. An army doctor and a psychologist attended to check our well-being. We were instructed not to mention the incident to anyone, not even the officers and soldiers.

Our statements were recorded in the truck on the way to the camp. Captain Sharma stationed two men outside to check on us. Our bags were checked and sent to us. I asked Varun about the car and the ammunition. He told me he didn't touch the car after the blast, and the rucksack was in the storeroom in the hotel. We felt restless.

'Who do you think is responsible for tonight?' I asked him.

'The crocodile,' he replied instantly. I felt he didn't even think about it and was expecting this question.

'But why would he get Viktor killed and me almost kidnapped? Moreover, I heard Wajahat, the helper, telling me that he wanted to keep me safe. However, he had a gun pointed at my head. I don't know. I guess there is someone else involved as well. Maybe it was the terror strike Viktor warned me against.'

'Are you sure?'

'I don't think Mr Bhat was involved.'

'Probably, you might have to put a gun to his head or his pants. He would definitely come out with the truth.'

'Pants?'

'Don't you know?'

'What?'

'The secret of Kashmir's self-proclaimed saviour.'

'I am all ears.'

'They say his only weakness is men,' he said and winked. For a second, I felt spellbound. I asked him twice if he was sure about it. He replied in the affirmative. I looked around at the things in the room. I wanted to think. I recollected Zeba Ji saying something along the same lines, which I had somehow ignored that day. Could Mr Bhat's sexual orientation be related to the conspiracy behind my father's accident?

I felt numb, not for the last time in the recent weeks. I asked Varun about his knowledge of the early '90s or Mr Bhat. We brainstormed about ideas related to the mystery of my father's demise. He told me about a few politicians who knew about Uncle's sexual orientation. He suspected that many under-the-table deals made in Kashmir were based on blackmailing Uncle into doing what the people in power deemed right.

'I don't even know that man's first name,' I sighed, feeling helpless.

'You should have asked Zeba Ji,' Varun replied.

'Shit. Yes, I should have. Don't you have any guesses, considering you might have heard from her or in the media circles?'

'The section of media that knew in depth about him is either retired or dead. There is no way of getting the information classified by the political corridors.'

'Classified? Are the files under lock and key?'

'Yes, they are. Physically, as well as digitally.'

'He lives like a dinosaur. He leaves imprints everywhere, but they are never traced back to him. We might need an army to get close to him,' I retorted, feeling a little demotivated.

'Absolutely not. Right now, he is at his weakest. The man who can save Kashmir from him is sitting right in front of me.'

'You are so kind. I am no hero. I am just a simple man willing to go the distance to know the truth.' I felt a tinge of hope in me. The excitement of last night was slowly ebbing away in this unnatural calm inside the army camp. I wanted to stretch my legs and go for a run. The rays of early morning sun were beginning to show on the other side of the camp.

I wanted to breathe in the early morning breeze and nourish my soul. With what I planned for the rest of the day, Kashmir might never be the same again, at least for me. Around six, the guards posted outside got tea with bread and butter. We weren't allowed near the mess.

'Why don't you listen to the audio Zeba Ji gave? You might get your answers about things that are bothering you,' Varun asked all of a sudden. We both felt energised after the tea. I had not been through a night in my recent memory. This, for a change, felt nostalgic, similar to the days of college.

'Oh, I completely forgot about that. Let's listen together,' I replied. As soon as we pressed play, I felt an adrenaline rush striking me. Varun, on the other hand, looked composed, as always.

The Morning of Gloom

As we were about to start the audio, one of the few working satellite phones in South Kashmir rang thrice. It was from a hotline number based in New Delhi. Bhat Saab jolted from his sleep. He rubbed his eyes, picked up the phone on the side table and said a meek hello.

'You are still sleepy, my friend,' the voice on the other end said.

'Yes, a little tired from last night.'

'What is the further course of action? Any new deputy coming up?'

'I'm still contemplating,' Mr Bhat replied. He was now fully awake. His grumpy mood started aching for a tea. Instead, he got up, went to the bar, picked up the half-empty bottle and poured himself some whiskey.

'Please be quick. The rush hour is approaching.'

'Be assured. I am fully aware of what is happening. You don't need to worry.'

'We need to be worried. Waves reach directly from Kashmir to New Delhi. Who better than you to understand?'

'This time, there shall be no waves. Everything has been shut from the top. Although I wasn't even consulted, yet I won't budge from my line of duty.'

'I expect nothing less from you. However, I need to answer my bosses. They don't want any mishaps after what transpired last night.'

'Let me handle it my way.'

'Of course. I didn't want to intrude. I was just calling to pay my condolences. I know how close the man was to you.'

'Thanks for your fake concern. Your condolences are accepted. Hope you enjoy your morning walk,' Mr Bhat said curtly and hung up.

The man sitting in New Delhi in his bungalow in Lutyens had a wry smile on his face. He got up, waved his personal assistant to bring his walking shoes and was about to set off for the daily routine. Mr Bhat, on the other hand, sat down on the deodar bench near the window. He opened the window sill and took a deep breath.

The breeze coming from the nearby river felt stale. The sounds of splashing water on the riverbank felt like a wave of ecstasy. He looked at the faraway mountains, lost in thought of what could have been. Viktor had to be given a farewell, but as per the protocol, he wasn't allowed anywhere near the body.

He sat in that position for more than an hour, reminiscing the memories of the last few years. His eyes, already puffy due to age, had started burning. Anger overwhelmed him for a moment as he threw his glass out of the window on the rocks. He looked at the pieces of glass being washed away by the river.

This was the only detoxification he did to wash away his memories. It had been the same since 1991. He decided to get fresh and live it as any other day. The fight in the name of Kashmir was still in his hands, and the political circus needed its master to be aware and alert.

A few minutes after Mr Bhat hung up, the same hotline number in Delhi called another satellite phone in South Kashmir. This time the person on the other side wasn't living in a bungalow sipping whiskey, instead he was offering the early morning prayers to God from an underground bunker.

He was lonely yet composed–long hair, white beard and wearing a torn phiran. He finished the prayers and let the phone ring. No one was allowed to disturb Sadiq Khan early in the morning.

A Call From Delhi

Twenty or thirty years from now, the Kashmir valley will see unprecedented tension. There would be people who might proclaim me as an astrologer for predicting the same, but son, don't believe them. They will tell you lie after lie. Do not take them to your heart. I speak directly to you, Raheel because I know that one fine day, you will come searching for the truth embedded in the tiniest corner in this world of lies.

Zeba Ji stands witness to me speaking this on the phone while she records. I can ensure you, as well as Zubeida, that no harm shall come to you. This might be the last phone call I am making to my motherland because I am aware of the threat to my life as well as yours. Long after I am gone far away, there will come a time when you, my son, will desperately seek answers.

Don't go any further than this iron-willed lady who has literally opened my eyes. You might also meet the master of webs–Aftab Bhat, commonly called Mr Bhat. He will recite verses, tell you stories and cry in your lap. Take my word for it, if you may, he is the vilest man alive. I am sure when you listen to this recording, your first reaction will be of surprise and the second of anguish, but you should have learned to channel your emotions, as your mother will. You will stand at a crossroads with many guiding lights but try to find the light that enlightens you from the inside and follow its path.

The audio paused for a few seconds. I looked at Varun, surprised and shaken. His eyes told me that he had already listened to this audio. His confidence was confusing me. Before I could entertain any other thoughts of my overthinking mind, a shrill female voice propped up.

Riyaz Ji, please don't stress yourself too much. You will be fine. I will always be there for you.

I know, Zeba Ji. My fear has automatically disappeared as we have progressed in this call.

Go ahead. The world awaits your ideas.

Before I go further, please promise that you shall wait for the right time and keep this safe with you.

Anything for you, Riyaz. You are a piece of my heart.

The recording paused again and restarted.

If you want to know more about Aftab Bhat, remember that the only time to get anything out of that man is when he is at his lowest. Strike when the iron is melting, but until then, please stay away and make your lives the only priority. I might sound crazy, but I already know how I will go. It will be a road accident, away from New Delhi or Kashmir. I do not know the date, but am aware that the transactions have happened.

Raheel, I now address you directly. When you listen to this, remember that all the secrets, tips and methods are a part of the tape that Aftab will hand over to you. He will try to decode those multiple times, but only you will understand the same. Do you know why? Because all those tips have emotions hidden in plain words.

My eyes started to moisten. I couldn't listen anymore. My vision was shaking. My mind was going back to my infant days. I paused the audio. Varun looked at me with empathy but didn't say a word. He understood that I needed space. Emotions had already suppressed my tipping point.

I felt like a rudderless boat tossed and turned by the gigantic waves of an ocean. I got up and went outside the room. The guards waved at me, asking me to go back in, but I paid no attention. I went towards the back of the room, which faced a forest, sat on a nearby rock and slumped down.

My head was hurting. I folded myself in a foetal position, held both my knees and cried. My sleeves were soon wet with my tears. I felt a slight touch on my left shoulder. One of the guards was looking at me, worried. He asked me if I was fine and needed anything. I smiled and thanked him. He went away, and my eyes started staring at the forest in front. The numb mind wanted nothingness.

Sometime later, Varun came, and I heard him speak to the guards. The sun, by now, was beginning to heat up a little. The early morning chirping of birds was growing louder. I regained my composure as Varun approached.

'Are you ok?'

'Yes, the outburst helped.'

'I'm sure,' he replied and smiled. He extended his hand to help me get up.

'Let's get back to work,' I said, rolling up my shirt sleeves and wiping my leftover tears. There was an audio to finish and a lot of information to be processed. We went inside and tapped the play button on the mobile. My world was about to turn upside down.

The Audio Again

If you ever get a chance to peek into Aftab Bhat's storeroom, try searching for a small brown colour wardrobe. The main wardrobe contains many important documents and information, but that small wardrobe contains secrets that he has kept classified from even the higher-ups. You might not know, but his house is under self-arranged 24-hour security.

So, if you, or anyone listening to me, thinks that taking him down and exposing this rotten system is easy, mark my words, it's not. I have always revered him like my own father, and he loved me in ways more than he should have. I am not going to talk about that, but I am sure, someday, Zeba Ji or someone else will fill in the details.

However, the way he is hell-bent on playing games with our nation by being hand in glove with all the parties with a stake in Kashmir has really appalled me. I have tried to bring his secrets out by exposing a politician and their shady deals, but I am not sure if that will cause any ripple effects.

Instead, by doing that, I have brought danger to everyone

I love. I am guilty of falling into his trap and assassinating many innocents. My hands are bloodied, but I want to give my soul a chance to repent.

Son, when you meet him, he will tell you a story about a high-ranking official giving a contract on my head. Aftab signed off that contract. To take out the best, you have to bring in the best. He has already tipped a man for my head. That man escaped the ambush laid by the security forces in Anantnag last year.

He is the most lethal terrorist ever to cross the border. I am sure by the time you hear this, Kashmir will be in turmoil, and the same man will be running the show. He might not come out in the open, but if he stays alive, there will be a bloodbath every year in the Valley. My problem is that terrorist has protection from the higher state agencies and is an asset to all the people involved. I cannot take him down alone. Nor can you. You will need someone trustworthy to finish this when the time comes.

I paused the audio yet again. My mind rushed to the small wardrobe I had seen at Bhat's residence. 'Who is this terrorist?' I asked Varun, hoping he had an answer.

'Sadiq Khan,' he replied.

'The one who has not been identified or seen by anyone.'

'Yes, precisely.'

'I have heard his name from Viktor. He is supposed to be the mastermind of all terror attacks.'

'You can confirm the same with Zeba Ji or your mother.'

'But does this mean that the threat Viktor and Mr Bhat have been talking about is real?'

'Yes, the threat is real. Even more authentic are their statements and mine about you being the only one who can save Kashmir.'

'How can I?'

'You will find that out yourself. Also, there are rumours that Sadiq is hiding in an underground tunnel or a cave somewhere in South Kashmir.'

'Why haven't our forces nailed him yet?'

'Because as Riyaz Ji said in the audio, he doesn't show up or come out. In addition, he has contacts everywhere. It's all a baseless rumour till he comes out or is dragged out.'

'Why will he come out?' I asked Varun. Curiosity was getting the better of me yet again. He didn't answer, instead kept looking at me.

'What? Why are you looking like that?'

'I am looking at the answer to your question,' he replied, leaving me stunned. I stumbled for words. I looked at him and then at my mobile. My father's words started haunting me.

Was I the pawn used to flush out the most dreaded terrorist ever to set foot in India? I started wondering.

'We should finish the audio. You need to chart the further course of action. We don't have much time,' Varun said, bringing me out of the web of questions. We played the audio again, this time for its last part.

The only way you can avenge me is by stopping the

barbaric terrorism that has crept inside the roots of Kashmir. For that, you will need to take out Aftab Bhat, Sadiq and all those officials whose names are on the secret documents kept safely in Bhat Saab's house. I know you will be able to accomplish what I wanted to.

Primarily because you would learn everything from Mr Bhat. Moreover, in the years to come, your mother will have planned everything, and when the time comes, she won't hesitate to take the shot.

Good luck, son.

This is Riyaz Dar, signing out on 26 November 1991.

There was a sound of a click. The sound of a landline disconnecting. A few seconds later, we heard heavy breathing; it was Zeba Ji. She had started crying like a child.

I will keep this safe for you, my child, till my dying breath, she said and wailed. The audio finished just like it had started. A lull before a storm, and a lull afterwards. There was silence in the room. My heartbeat was racing. A storm was about to engulf everyone I knew.

The Cat and Mouse Chase

August 2019

A mobile phone vibrated on Zeba Ji's dining table. She answered but did not speak. She had found the phone in the field outside, 200 metres away from her house, near the dead sniper's body.

'Is the work over?' the voice on the phone asked. She kept quiet. She listened intently to the voice modulated on the other end. 'Why the hell aren't you answering?' the hoarse voice asked again.

'Because he cannot speak any longer,' Zeba Ji spoke slowly, playing with her voice a little. The caller hung up. She knew where the call was from and had no inclination to work more towards it. She asked Zubeida to serve her the tea. They planned to grab some breakfast and leave the place.

A Maruti 800 was already parked outside. Her trusted helper had arrived 20 minutes back. The helper was trying to convince Zeba Ji to hide at his house. Everyone in the area revered her. Her house at the hilltop being a scenic spot, children of the villagers would often flock around. This is where she first met Tariq, the helper, 15 years back.

She grew fond of him and found solace in his presence. Having never married, she always wanted to have a son. For the last 15 years, Tariq had filled that void. As they headed out, Tariq carried their bags. Zeba Ji and Zubeida dragged a brown rucksack into the trunk of the car.

She wasn't expecting to use the Scorpio TGT but didn't want to take any chances. Having covered some distance, Zubeida rolled down the window and let the morning air fill her senses.

'I have already spoken to my uncle. He lives on the outskirts of Bijbehara. You will be safe there,' Tariq blurted. He spoke fast while trying to concentrate on the curved roads ahead.

'I'm not sure about that. It will be too near to where that man is,' Zeba Ji replied.

'Where are you planning to hide then?'

'How far is your uncle's place from Aftab's house?' Zubeida cut in.

'Around 5 Km,' Tariq responded.

'Let's go then, but on one condition. You will help me with the path towards his house.'

'I can do that with closed eyes. I know the way by heart.'

'He has been keeping an eye on him for the last two years. He is the guy I trust with my life,' Zeba Ji spoke up. The next 20 Km were full of passes. Zubeida stared at the trees on the hilltops. The villages she once called home seemed alien to her observant eyes. She was engrossed in deep thought. The revenge she had hidden all these years was finally consuming her.

The contract on Zeba Ji's name had not yet expired. Two motorcycle-borne youths started from Anantnag towards Tral at the same time as Tariq was driving Zeba Ji and Zubeida away. Aftab Bhat was pained at hearing his sister's voice. The bikers had instructions to rush and cover the 30-Km distance as fast as possible.

The woman he wanted dead all these years had eluded yet another attempt on her life. He was trying to get in touch with the Commanding Officer of the RR unit but couldn't. Frustrated, he banged his phone on the floor.

'Why isn't any fucking thing happening right?' he yelled. His servant, who had arrived early morning, came running towards his room. He had this habit of being too attentive to his master's call. Aftab Bhat shooed him away. He wasn't interested in entertaining anyone. He was trying to contemplate the methods of his sister. How did she win every time he tried to get her case? Why is it that since childhood, she has humiliated him in every way possible?

An hour later, Mushtaq, one of the bikers he had sent to Tral, called back. He informed that Zeba Ji's house was empty. Aftab felt a lump in his throat.

'Have you checked the whole premise?' he asked.

'Yes, Sir. No one is around. However, her stuff is all here. Nothing seems amiss. Probably she has gone out somewhere,' Mushtaq responded tentatively, scared of irritating his master.

'You fool. Where would an old woman go at eight in the morning? Come back. Hide where you have been hiding, and tell your leader that danger is lurking.'

The manager of the political circus in Kashmir for over three decades was beginning to feel scared of an old woman. The woman who had taught him everything and retired from active operations many years back. Shit was getting deeper. He realised he did not have any trustworthy men left. With Viktor gone, there was no one he could talk to and influence. Apart from maybe one guy, who he thought he could call his own.

'It's time to bring Riyaz's son into the game,' he muttered.

The Impending Visit

2 September

Aftab Bhat finished his usual breakfast of boiled egg and toast with coffee. He prepared himself to make a few more calls. No one from the RR unit had responded since early morning. In between multiple calls from the capital, he instructed his team to ensure a proper burial for Viktor.

He didn't want to leave any stone unturned for the man he loved so dearly. The enormous wall clock made a bugle sound ten times. The sun's rays were seeping in through the curtains.

Tariq dropped Zeba Ji at his uncle's house and continued towards Aftab's residence with Zubeida. They reached a small settlement in the middle of an apple orchard that overlooked the uncle's house. It was merely 500 m but hidden from plain sight. While approaching the orchard, Tariq informed Zubeida about the different security personnel around.

Two burly men who constantly sat at a nearby teashop. A particular sweeper who was always loitering around the nearby lanes. The last and the most important is the farmer in the orchard just beside Mr Bhat's house.

'Can you fetch the scope from the bag, please? It's in the back of your car,' Zubeida asked politely.

'Sure. I will be right back.' Tariq returned with the grey-coloured scope, which Zubeida used judiciously for the next 30 minutes. She checked Aftab Bhat's house and the layers of security from all possible angles. She had a small notepad to fill in the details. She had this habit of noting down things from her teaching days. Oblivious to the fact that his air of arrogance was being scrutinised from a nearby orchard, Mr Bhat dialled the RR unit again.

'I want to speak to the civilian you picked up from Hotel Paramount last night,' he yelled.

'We will arrange a call back soon, Sir.'

'You have told me the same thing five times. Don't you know who I am?'

'No Sir, I don't,' the operator, Lance Naik Tek Chand politely answered and hung up. He went straight to Captain Sharma and informed him about the call. There was something about Aftab that even the security forces started getting weak knees. He was always arranging phone calls directly from New Delhi and using undue pressure to accomplish things. Captain Sharma quickly came to our room.

'He has called five times, starting early morning at 6.'

'Don't worry, we are ready for him,' I replied.

'You need to act quickly. We are leaving for combing operations around Anantnag. We can drop you on the way if you are planning anything.'

'Let me call him first,' I said, and looked at Varun. He nodded slightly. Captain gave me his satellite phone. I called Zeba Ji first and told her about my plans. She said that she felt proud of me and wished me luck. She told me that my mother had gone to do a recon of Aftab Bhat's house. I couldn't fathom why. She provided me the directions to the place where they were holding up. I called up Mr Bhat. His satellite phone rang twice.

'Hi, Raheel,' he spoke slowly. He already knew that it was me on the other side. The man never ceased to amaze me.

'You seem low. Are you fine?'

'Yes, I am holding up well. How about you?'

'I am ok. Hope you are at your home today. I will come and see you.'

'Sure, I will have *Kehwa* prepared for you,' he replied, and we hung up. Half an hour later, the team was ready. We asked them to drop us near Dal, as we had some unfinished business. We reached Varun's hotel, met the receptionist and got the keys to the storeroom.

After picking up the rucksack, we rushed back. The receptionist looked at Varun and nodded in affirmation. We quickly moved towards the car. My legs started shivering as I sat on the passenger's seat.

The Stride Ahead

On the way, the security forces stopped us at two checkpoints. Both of us were nervous, as we were carrying weapons. Fortunately, we did not have to argue much with any of the soldiers. We reached our destination in an hour. Mother hugged me tight, and Zeba Ji patted my shoulder.

'You have become weak in a night,' she said and smiled.

'Have a seat, brother, I will get something to eat,' Tariq cut in.

'Please get us some tea.'

'Sure. I will get tea for everyone,' he responded and left. Mum came towards me, held my hand slightly and asked if I was ready. I nodded but did not say anything. I felt emotions were getting the better of her. Varun was standing right behind me, silently looking at us. Zeba Ji asked him to pull the sofa seats towards us.

I sat upright, trying to control my nervousness with every ounce of strength I possessed. My mother and Zeba Ji tried to give a pep talk to keep my mind from overthinking. In about ten minutes, Tariq returned with a tray full of biscuits and snacks. Alongside him was a young woman holding the tray with teapot and cups.

She had covered herself with a veil, but her eyes were shining. In that moment of fear and weakness, my eyes met hers, and I felt a strange emotion pass through me. I looked at her for a second too long when Varun started coughing. Coming back to my senses, I got up and helped Tariq arrange everything on the table.

'How are you, my child?' Zeba Ji asked the woman.

'I am fine with your blessings,' she replied quickly, poured tea into the cups and left. As I picked up the cup of tea and tasted the first sip, a thought gathered pace on my inside. I had seen these eyes somewhere. Tariq offered me the plate of biscuits, but my mind was elsewhere.

'Raheel,' Varun called out. 'Where are you?'

'No, nothing. I was just thinking something,' I replied, dusting my overthinking mind with another sip of tea. I picked a biscuit from the plate, as Tariq's hand was still outstretched.

'You don't need to think much. These feisty women here, they will take care of everything,' Tariq interrupted and smiled, looking at Zeba Ji. I had forgotten to ask my mother why she had gone for a recon of Mr Bhat's house, and Tariq's statement shed light on the same.

I smiled and replied in affirmation. My thoughts

veered towards Aftab Bhat. *How was I going to face him and his overwhelming persona?* I wondered. I was way off the track from being even an amateur spy. My overtly confused mind started troubling again. Half an hour later, all of them wished me luck.

Tariq was to drop me near Aftab's place, and Varun was planning to walk a separate path towards a tea stall nearby. He dropped me at the main road. I got off and slowly walked towards my destination. During our ten-minute drive, Tariq quickly filled in the details about the men who would be keeping an eye on me.

The bearded burly men at the tea stall on the main road, the sweeper and the farmer. There were nine houses till Bhat Uncle's house from the main road. As I walked, I felt someone continuously watching me. The automatic revolver was buckled tight. A spare magazine taped to my right sock. My body was ready to embrace the truth and path of revenge. But was my mind and soul up for it?

Father of Spies

He was standing near the edge of his first-floor balcony, eyes piercing my every movement. I turned the corner towards his entrance, and thc gatekeeper greeted me warmly. I smiled back. The sun was at its brightest. I narrowed my eyes, looked up towards Aftab and waved. He signalled me to head upstairs.

I took slow, measured steps. On the stairs, I tried to peek inside the storeroom to check the small brown wardrobe. The door was shut. Mr Bhat moved quickly towards me and embraced. He asked about my well-being.

'I am sorry you had to go through all this,' he said.

'It's fine. I am slowly getting used to this place,' I replied. My instinct told me that he didn't know anything about my mother being present around the area or about Zeba Ji.

'Did you speak to Viktor…umm…before he was

assassinated?' He asked, fumbling for words.

'I did. He told me about a threat to my life as well as his. Someone had tipped him off about an attack. I am sorry for your loss. Viktor was a really good guy.'

'And the second best in my team ever. The best still happens to be Riyaz,' he mentioned my father's name with moist eyes. He wiped his face with a hand towel. I tapped his shoulder and assured him of my support.

'If you have any other input, you can share it with me. I will try to work on it to the best of my ability.'

'I have already informed the RR team. I hope he told you about the search operation. It was based on my tip only,' he replied. I started thinking at double speed. Had Aftab already given away Sadiq's location, even though he was the most protected terrorist in Kashmir? If not, who exactly was Captain Sharma after? At that moment, his servant showed up with tea.

The aroma of *Kehwa* awakened my senses and calmed me down. His overwhelming presence, which had affected my confidence initially, was beginning to wear out. I was tapping my right foot with each sip. I had to overcome the nervousness at any cost and ask him important questions.

'Did you inform the RR unit about Sadiq?' I asked abruptly. He stared at me for a moment longer than usual, and I could figure out he was surprised. He narrowed his eyes to look into mine.

'Which Sadiq are you talking about?' He questioned back.

'The one responsible for the murder of your best teammate,' I replied and left him gasping for breath. The saucer in his fingers started shaking. He gulped hard, the sip of tea stuck in his throat. He was searching for words to reply. He managed to stretch and keep the saucer on the table. I had finally managed to shake the confidence of the father of spies in Kashmir. It was the moment of reckoning, the moment to strike hard. I started speaking again.

'You might not agree with me, but I have listened to an audio of my father, and I have formed an opinion about you and everyone else who runs the system. I feel everything here is rotten beyond repair. You never told me the name of the man my father brought in from the other side, the bastard, you said, betrayed him. Here I am telling you his name and seeing you go white as if you have seen a ghost.'

'You have no idea what trap you are falling into. You seem to have been brainwashed. I need to clarify all your doubts. Sadiq might be a terrorist in your or anyone's language, but for me, he's an asset. Do you even know about his operations that have helped us?'

'Operations? Probably, you should clear my doubt about the non-existent Operation Lidder of 1988-89. The story of the mission you had filled my ears with. Wasn't that a concocted lie?'

'Who told you all this?'

'An audio recording of the man you call your best teammate.'

'He wasn't just my best teammate, dammit. I loved him like anything. He was more than a son to me,' he shouted, held his forehead with his left hand and slowly started crying.

'Yes, he was the only lover you ever had, apart from Viktor,' I cut in, leaving him in shock. He gripped the arms of his chair and slumped back. He looked at me with sunken eyes. He tried speaking, but nothing escaped his parched throat. He started breathing heavily and signalled me to pass him the water bottle on the dining table.

I had successfully made the first move. I slowly got up and went towards the dining table. I handed him a glass and water and asked him to take deep breaths. I felt he was hit by a bout of nervousness, so heavy that his whole persona lay shattered in front of me. He gulped two glasses of water quickly and told me to take a seat. Resting his head on the chair, he started rocking it.

'Did you meet my sister?' He asked in a measured tone.

'Do you have a sister as well?' I counter questioned. I wasn't willing to relent to this man. I looked back with fierceness. A few weeks in Kashmir, and I had learned how to control my body language.

'The statements you are making today haven't surprised me. You just proved what I was thinking all along. You, that journalist and my lovely sister. The three of you have been hatching a plan to eliminate me. What does she want? Is she planning to get someone in my place from Delhi? Did she tell you about her lovers based in the national capital?' Aftab Bhat was fuming.

'I have no idea what you are talking about. Whatever little I know is from the audio tapes I have listened to. The one you gave me was only the instructions part. I received an audio from Jahangir. I had gone to ask him for help with the task assigned to me by Viktor. I managed to earn the trust of a few men around Dal, and Jahangir was instrumental in the same. He gave me an audio that apparently was with him since November 1991. Hope you remember what transpired then?'

'Jahangir is a motherfucker. He has played you. I'm sure he has been paid to give that audio to you.'

'By whom?'

'I will get to know. You don't need to worry.'

'I am worried about you. You are sweating. The air of confidence around you has vanished. Your overwhelming personality has given way to a confused old man who is just shooting arrows into a dark alley without knowing where his target is,' I said and got up. I turned towards the balcony and let the view linger in front of my eyes.

'I will take care of you, son,' he mumbled, standing a foot away. I was taken aback. He had got up and moved towards me without me even realising. I took a step further. In a rush of blood, I turned around and shoved him away.

'Don't dare come near me,' I shouted. He stopped in his tracks. An inch more, and I would have pushed him hard.

'Sure, let's just talk,' he replied, calm, just like he always used to.

'I will. But before that, you need to answer my questions.'

'Go on.'

'Does the small wardrobe in your store have important documents? The ones that even the people in power are not supposed to see.'

'No, not at all.' He stressed too much about rejecting my claim and gave the truth away. He was trying to shrug off the pinch of nervousness, but sometimes things get beyond our control. I stared back and smiled. In that instant, he realised I had caught him lying. His facial muscles clenched, and his palms started sweating.

The man, who saw through me three weeks ago, was lowering his guard in front of me. I anxiously waited for him to make the fatal mistake. I knew he would.

The Veiled Woman

Aftab Bhat slowly got up from his chair and headed towards the bar cabinet. He walked like an old, broken man. My eyes followed him all the way until he squatted and opened the bottom drawer. The drawer creaked, and a millisecond later, a metal-like object clanked.

He turned around and pointed his revolver at me. He took a few steps to his left and stood near the balcony door, keeping the gun pointed at me. My left hand slowly went towards the back of my jeans.

'Don't even try. I will blow your brains,' he threatened. I looked right at him, showing him my hands kept above my head.

'I was hoping for a staged accident in a remote location in Kashmir. Like you did with your favourite lover and the best teammate.'

'Shut up, you fool. You know nothing,' he yelled and lowered the gun for an instant. 'You think I got your father killed. Go on and put a bullet through me. I am standing right here. Come on, take your revenge.'

When someone tells you to draw your gun and avenge a murder, remember they are playing with your mind. Better to demoralise them with your words and eyes before they gather the courage to pull the trigger. Father's tips from the audio echoed in my mind.

'Do you think I have come alone?' I asked a quick question, making him look around the windows towards the orchards and farms.

'You don't play games with me.'

'I am not playing a game, Mr Aftab Bhat,' I said, sending shivers down his spine. He took a step back towards the window. I realised he wanted support to maintain his balance. I stood up, unarmed and took a step towards him. He moved further back, trying to grab the windowsill with his left hand and redrew his gun, pointing it at me with his right.

I moved ahead and sidestepped quickly. He aimed and pulled the trigger. The bullet whizzed past my ear, but he lost his balance on the recoil. I pulled my revolver out and shot straight at his arm. It hit his right wrist. Blood started oozing out of his wound as he growled in pain. He fell on his knees, clutching his right hand with his left. He grimaced and hurled expletives at me.

At that instant, there was a flash of lightning right behind him. A second later, a loud bang echoed, the sound of a sniper hitting the target. Two more shots came about in the next five seconds as I heard people running from the shop just outside the lane towards Mr Bhat's residence. Another two rounds were fired in the next one minute, and a demonic silence followed.

In the middle of the apple orchard that overlooked the house, a veiled woman got up from her position. She slowly dismantled the Scorpio TGT rifle and kept it carefully in the rucksack. She smiled satisfactorily, looking at the carnage she had just caused. Six shots, out of which three were headshots, killing Aftab Bhat's servant, his personal security officer (the farmer) and the roadside sweeper in an instant.

The men who came running from the tea stall also fell prey to the .338 Magnum rounds piercing their necks. Tariq was waiting right below the settlement. He was nervous and biting his nails. Zubcida rushed downstairs, lifted the veil and smiled at him. They ran towards his car, and he sped back to his uncle's house. She nodded in affirmation, looking at Varun, who was standing near the tea stall.

He had a small cup of tea in his hand. Everyone around the stall had run away. As they left the area behind, Zubeida slid sideways out of the seat, extended her shoulders out of the window and embraced the bright, sunny day. Breathing heavily, she believed that she had avenged her husband.

A Fallen Master

As his men fell to the sniper one by one, Aftab tried to get up and check what was happening. The pain engulfed him. He couldn't gather the courage to stand on his feet. I went near him and picked up his revolver. The man who ruled the crown of India for so many years could not be trusted. The least I wanted at that moment was a confession. I prodded his ribs and made him lie on his back. He was clutching his arm and losing blood.

'Tell me the truth,' I yelled at his face.

'I have told you everything,' he replied.

'Either you are lying, or everything that my father spoke in the audio was a lie. Which one should I trust? The voice of the man who gave me his blood, or the one who is losing blood right now.'

'I will tell you everything. You can ask whatever you want. Please save me. I don't want to die like this. I am feeling dizzy,' he pleaded.

'That's good. Remember the dizziness my father would have faced after that accident,' I shouted. My voice was stern.

'I have already told you that the man behind that conspiracy is dead.'

'Do you have proof that the same man got my father killed? I have an audio tape dated 26 November 1991 wherein my father clearly states that it was you who started the contract on his head. Do you remember that date? It was the last night my father must have seen his favourite muse, the moon.'

'I do. We lost him the next day.' He began to cry. Using his left elbow as support on the floor, he tried to sit straight, his back supported by the wall. He looked at me with the eyes of a man who had lost everything, even his will to fight. I sat down cross-legged in front of him. My neck had started hurting.

'It was me. He had gone rogue and shared secrets with ISI and Pakistan-sponsored terror organisations. I couldn't take the heartbreak he gave me when he married your mother. After you were born, he drifted further away. I wanted him back at any cost, but he started blackmailing me. He knew far too much for me to handle. His actions had to be dealt with.'

'And yet you say you loved him? Disgraceful, you are,' I shouted, pointing my index finger at his eyes.

'I did. I swear to God. The people in power forced my hand. My own heartache could have been controlled, but when I got that fateful call on 20 November 1991, I couldn't do anything.'

'What did they say?'

'They had our secrets. His dealings with ISI were out in the open. Many in the bureaucracy knew about him being rogue.'

'Shut up, Aftab Bhat. My father was a patriot. He was the bravest man you ever met. These are your own words and yet you have the balls to call him rogue. Have some shame.'

'He was always rogue. He was never under my control.' His words pierced my bones like a curved dagger inching upwards towards my heart. I felt pain ringing in my head. I wanted to crush him to death for bad-mouthing my hero. My arms felt a rush of blood, but I controlled myself. I wanted to probe this demon till his last breath. He was dying anyway.

'But you loved him. You could have ensured he returned to the right path like you did in the past,' I asked.

'I tried, before enabling the contract on his head. He didn't relent. I tried my best, but he was hell-bent on destroying the very system that made him in the first place.'

'And you allowed Sadiq to take him down. Later, you and your masters protected the killer of my father.'

'Yes,' he replied. His voice was full of hesitation. 'I regret it every single day. Today, as we speak, Sadiq is totally out of my control and is planning multiple strikes across the state.'

'No, you don't.' I cut him short. 'You will regret when you are at your rightful place in hell while I destroy the system you carefully built. This rotten piece of governance and false calm that you project the Kashmir valley has always been in; I will tear it all apart.' I looked right in his eyes. His face turned pale. I relished his pain. He clenched his injured hand and forced himself into a pleading position with folded hands.

'Make the next minute my last, I beg you.' He began to sob uncontrollably.

'One last question. Why did you send me the letters and email to force me to come here?'

'What letters? I didn't send you anything. You wanted to come to Kashmir. Zeba conveyed the same to me. I just saw you as the heir to Riyaz.'

'To do what?'

'To finish what your father started. Save the Kashmir valley. I wasn't able to do it alone. Neither could have Viktor.'

'To hell with Kashmir. I had no idea what it looked like before I got here. Everything is about your interests. What about the truth I seek? Aren't you Mr Sharma? Those letters and emails had a common sender, Mr Yoginder Sharma from Solan.' His face turned red.

'What the hell? That was the code name only used during my secret interactions with your father. Only Riyaz called me by that name personally. No one else,' he replied, leaving me in disbelief. Could this mean that there was someone else and all this while I was after Mr

Bhat to find the truth? My eyes were transfixed at his. My mind was overthinking about the possibilities.

'Let me help one last time,' he said with a trembling voice. He asked me to fetch his satellite phone. Supported on his elbows, he dialled a number and asked the receiver to stay at his hideout.

'Riyaz's son is coming after you. The army will also come. Stay where you are,' he spoke softly and hung up. Slowly, he clenched his teeth and turned a little. He used his left hand to feel something in his right pocket. My fingers tightened around the trigger. He fetched a key from his trousers and offered me his outstretched palm.

'Take it. You will find his address here. Also, make my death a little less painful,' he mumbled, having lost all his strength. I went towards him, held his hands tight one last time and bid him goodbye. I pointed my gun at his temple a few seconds later. He closed his eyes, ready for me to pull the trigger.

I stared on, heartless, like my father had been once. My legs did not shiver; my hands were steady. A flash of light, slight recoil and a spurt of blood covered my face and clothes. The story of Aftab Bhat finished, and in my left palm lay the keys that would unravel the gory truth of Kashmir over the last thirty years.

The Small Wardrobe

With three clicks and a small push, the wardrobe opened with a light thud. The papers were stacked neatly in different columns. The ones in the bottom-most corner were yellowish. They seemed older than the rest. I decided to begin there. One by one, I used my phone to click a picture.

Some had illegible handwriting, but the others were crisp and clear. Pictures of porous border areas in North Kashmir, names of security personnel whom I believed were now already retired. Some of them contained security details of separatist leaders and the names of common people, probably social workers or journalists.

A few were financial transactions of payment deposited in international accounts. After checking around ten similar documents, I noticed a pattern. The names of the receiving account holder and the depositor were the same. Depositor-Aftab Bhat and Recipient-Sadiq Khan. My worst fears were coming true. The documented proof was right in front of my eyes.

The state was helping a terrorist, and Mr Bhat was at its forefront. After rummaging through random documents, I laid my hands on the most important information. The safe houses that Aftab Bhat and his team had. There were three in South Kashmir. A total of twenty in the Kashmir valley.

I was trying to comprehend what to do with the papers and information when I heard someone calling my name. It was Varun. He was standing near the stairs on the ground floor.

'Get the fuck out of here,' he spoke fast. For the first time, I had seen the monk-like man lose his shit.

'Have you brought the bag?' I asked. He ran a few steps up and threw a carry bag in my direction. I quickly collected some papers and pushed them in. It was impossible to take everything from the wardrobe. I went with my instincts. Varun kept a close watch on the gate and the lane outside. I rushed down but stopped midway.

I had forgotten my revolver near the bar table where Aftab lay dead. I picked up the gun as well as the two phones lying there. Varun came running and asked me to use a towel or handkerchief to wipe the fingerprints. Shamelessly, we used an eighteen-year-old Johnnie Walker from the bar cabinet. In two minutes, we were ready to leave.

'RR unit is approaching from the main road. We need to run into the nearby forest,' Varun spoke quickly as he tapped my shoulder, giving me directions.

'With this bag?'

'Yes. Do you intend to get yourself shot?'

'We can meet the RR unit. It must be Captain Sharma leading the team,' I tried to reason with him.

'No, it's his boss, along with the SOG of J and K Police.'

'How do you know all this?' I asked, without looking at him. I was already panting for breath. The bag was heavier than expected.

'I called the police to report the shooting. I also called Sharma and told him everything. He is the only person we both should trust. Now, fuck everything and run.'

'What the hell?' I yelled as we continued to run deep into the forest. We heard the vehicles approaching the area. I had spent 15 minutes inside Bhat Niwas from the time the first bullet was shot. Either the SOG was too busy in the combing operation, or the threat perception around Aftab had gone down considerably.

Either way, it held us in good stead. We had a head start, and the dense forest was our advantage. On the other side of the forest were apple meadows and a semi-constructed road. Varun signalled towards the road. We continued running until we reached the road. We looked around and went further.

The road curved towards the left, moving between meadows. A kilometre ahead, I noticed a white Maruti 800 with a man in the driver's seat. I stopped in my tracks while Varun continued walking. He looked over his shoulder towards me and suggested we keep at it.

'There is our escape,' he exclaimed, pointing towards the vehicle. As we moved further, I noticed Tariq waving at us. I smiled for the first time in the last few hours. We had achieved the first objective. Varun patted my back while Tariq congratulated me. They seemed content with what we had achieved. I, on the other hand, was still grappling with the truth on the path of satisfaction.

Tariq drove slowly towards his uncle's house. Five minutes later, he received a call on his mobile. A series of bomb blasts had ripped apart Kashmir. Lal Chowk, some cantonment areas, Gulshan Dhaba and other areas were targeted. Some civilians were injured around Lal Chowk, while some CRPF men sustained minor scratches at Gulshan's. Unfortunately, we lost Jahangir.

Reluctantly, I asked both of them about the person who shot dead all the guards. They did not reply, but I knew who it was.

Zeba Ji and my mother were pacing around the house when we reached. Mother came running towards me and embraced me. Tears started flowing freely as she kissed my forehead. She was still wearing the veil. The one she wore while killing five men in broad daylight.

'It was me,' she murmured, crying and smiling at the same time. Her shivering hands were rubbing my face lovingly. The fierce nature of the woman behind the veil and the motherly instincts were poles apart. She wanted to protect her child at all costs and was ready to sacrifice anything in her path. My heart was unable to bear the fact that my mother could actually kill someone.

Beginning of the End

After a while, everyone's mobiles started ringing. Bomb blasts, the killing of Aftab Bhat, a robbery at his house, and the killing of his staff had sent the RR unit and J and K police on a hunt. Varun received a call from Captain Sharma. His face turned pale, listening to Captain's words.

He knew about our mission and informed us that all the higher authorities had been involved. The unofficial command of Indian Intelligence was ripped apart in less than twelve hours. Zeba Ji received multiple calls from New Delhi, informing her about the situation in the national capital. The top chairs were worried. Kashmir was slipping out of their hands.

A source informed Tariq about an imminent crackdown in the entire South Kashmir. Although Aftab Bhat did not have an official position, he controlled everything with the word Kashmir. Viktor, on the other hand, worked for the government and reported to Mr Bhat bypassing the actual chief of Intelligence in Kashmir.

The state was put on an alert. Despite the presence of lakhs of security men in the valley, random terror attacks and killings have sent shock waves across the country's media.

Zeba Ji asked Tariq to dispose of the car and the sniper rifle in the fields or the nearby orchards. He quickly went off to work. She asked us to sit around the dining table and carefully unpack the bag with papers. We had to hatch a plan to get the security forces to look in different directions.

An hour later, photographs of old documents regarding financial transactions between separatist leaders, security forces, and politicians surfaced on Twitter, the buzzing social media application. Around a hundred characters with ten pictures were enough to set the ball rolling. Questions were asked of the entire political class across the country.

Politicians from the previous government, retired defence personnel, and some current ministers were brought under the scanner by the media. She passed two sheets towards my side and asked me to scrutinise them. They were the safe houses that she suspected Sadiq might be in. Mother asked me to trust my own instincts.

A phone call to Zeba Ji from someone in the CBI confirmed that arrest warrants had been issued against five people, and the arrests would be made the same evening. The man who had called Aftab Bhat on the satellite phone early morning wasn't on this list.

'We are almost there, Riyaz Ji,' she whispered, looking at the blue skies outside. The afternoon had begun to set in. I was hungry but eager to embark on my final journey of truth. Zubeida brought some more tea, and this time, I did not suspect her eyes. I got a pen from a diary on the side table and wrote down two locations on a piece of paper.

I kept the paper in front of my mother and asked her to point me to one. She looked at the paper, and emotions swelled up once again. Her fingers stroked the paper where the location was written, Sun Temple, Mattan. 'This is where I first met your father,' she admitted and smiled. Her glistening tears left soft imprints on the happy dimples.

I asked Tariq's uncle if I could borrow his scooter. The journey towards truth was about 12 Km long, and Zeba Ji specifically mentioned avoiding the highways and the security pickets.

'Keep that VIP pass inside your pockets and stay alive,' my mother advised as I was about to leave.

'Make *Kehwa* for me when I return,' I replied. We hugged and cried out aloud.

The End

The late afternoon breeze tantalised my skin. I was riding a scooter after nearly a decade. Avoiding the highway, I zoomed through the village roads. The smell of wet mud from the apple orchards refreshed my senses. A few convoys passed by from the opposite side. The surrounding villagers looked a little relaxed.

I attached two milk containers to either side of the scooter. In Kashmir, it is always better to expect the unexpected. After riding slowly for 30 minutes, I entered Mattan and was stopped at a picket. They casually asked me about my destination and let me go looking at the milk containers and my unkempt beard.

I didn't know my mother was so adept at creating a milkman out of a corporate employee turned part-time spy. I parked the scooter at a distance from the temple, near a house, which had a few children playing outside. I decided to go further on foot. Going through the by-lanes, I arrived behind the house I was looking for.

It was a desolate stretch. I realised that Sadiq wouldn't be holding up inside the magnanimous house and tried to look around for clues. After a few minutes, I saw a dilapidated house towards the right and a small shed at its entry. Before moving ahead, I stood there for a few seconds, trying to check if anyone was following. There was a thick covering of grass right next to the shed.

It was unnatural and grabbed my attention. I tried to stomp on it, but my right foot went through. Quickly taking a step back, I drew my gun. All this time, it was buckled around my right calf. In slow motion, I removed the grass covering and stepped inside. It was an underground bunker with a staircase. The silence was deafening.

The nearest security picket was a kilometre away. I wanted to do this all by myself. It was time to utilise whatever I had learned. I drew my Glock 17 at my eye line. It was dark, but I avoided using my mobile torch. Having taken ten steps inside, the sound of a slight cough startled me.

It seemed someone was trying to suppress the noise with his arm. I grabbed my mobile in my left hand and moved towards the noise, ready to shine the torch and catch them by surprise.

There was a sharp left, which led to a small room. It was illuminated by what looked like a night bulb. From my position, I managed to see two shadows, standing men, probably. As I moved further in the demonic silence,

I overheard the slight click of a gun being unlocked. The bulb went off.

A second later, a burst of fire forced me to jump for cover. A flash of pain engulfed my left cheek. It was bloody but manageable. My skin felt like a hot flash pan. The bullet had grazed me. An inch to the left, and I would have been dead. I quickly sprang into position. Back to the wall, covered by a pillar, gun drawn forward.

Footsteps approached as I waited anxiously. In hushed voices, the two shadows argued about who would take the lead. They waited for me to make the move; I didn't flinch. After thirty seconds, I heard a hoarse voice coming from inside.

'Get back in, you fools,' the voice thundered. In muffled voices, the men who were just ten feet away from me started arguing again. I took the chance. They turned around to head back into the room. I turned the gun's safety off, switched it to burst mode and inched ahead.

'Motherfuckers,' I screamed as I pressed the trigger, sending a burst of three shots in a swift motion. The one on the right was hit in the face. He collapsed on the spot. The other jumped inside. I shot another burst. The bullet whizzed right through his knee, and he let out a wail. I ran towards him. Before he could pick up his automatic, I shot through his neck. Instantly, I heard a clap. I stopped in my tracks.

'Whoa. Dramatic entry. Come in, I won't hurt you.' The same thunderous voice came again. I mustered courage and went in. Gun drawn, looking for shadows in the dark room. My eyes narrowed with extreme focus. He switched on the bulb, with a small button in his hand. An AK47 was lying to his left, and a revolver to his right.

He was sitting straight, cross-legged, his hands splayed on either side, ready to pick up the gun and shoot any moment. His face seemed frail, but his eyes were sparkling as if on fire. Something in those eyes seemed familiar. I had seen them, maybe in a picture. The flowing beard made him look more daunting than Aftab Bhat. I quickly pointed my gun towards him.

'Don't move your hands. Keep them on your knees,' I yelled. My voice echoed. He smiled. My heart was beating faster than a train, and this man was calm like a monk.

'Put your gun down, son. You don't have to kill me. I am the man whose truth you seek,' he spoke softly. His words were measured as if his tongue had a weighing scale. I was bewildered. *Was he playing a game, or was it something else?* I thought to myself.

'Sadiq Khan, you killed my father. I am not letting you out alive today,' I clenched my facial muscles and said aloud. My body was shaking, but I wanted an air of confidence around me. He smirked and started laughing, looking at me.

'You still don't get it. Do you?'

'What?' I said, perplexed.

'Listen to me carefully. The nearby army unit has already heard the chaotic sounds of bullets. They must have cordoned off the area. When I die, as I will in the next 30 seconds, take the letter from my right pocket, move out from the right and go away. Do not look back,' he said, pointing to a small wooden opening on my left.

'And why will I take your advice?' I asked, raging with anger at the sheer audacity of this terrorist. He stared at me and moved his hands through his wavy hair.

'Because I am the man whom you were searching for in Solan,' he replied. His voice shaking. The words clattered my mind and body as if a thousand clubs were beating me. I couldn't think straight. Aftab Bhat's words came ringing back. No one apart from him and my father knew about the name, Yoginder Sharma from Solan. I shut my eyes for a moment to surmise the situation.

My gun was automatically lowered. The sheer vehemence of the moment weakened my knees. I opened my eyes to see Riyaz Dar smiling with his arms wide open, inviting me for a hug. I jumped onto the mattress he was sitting on, embraced him, and started crying. He held me tight.

'Stay safe, my child,' he said gently. He held my face in his hands and kissed my forehead. The next moment, he used both his hands to push me ferociously. I fell on my back a foot away from the mattress. As I got up, I saw him looking at the roof. The revolver, in his right hand, pushed firmly against the base of his jaw.

His eyes closed. His lips slightly parted as if praying one last time. A millisecond later, my life was back to square one. A flash of light and blood all over. The man, who died in a road accident 30 years ago, was lying in front of me with his brain rammed out. I fell to my knees, staring at his lifeless body. My heart had only one question, 'why?'

The Final Letter

Dear Son,
Today, as my time nears, I write this last letter to you.

The man they think I am died in that fateful road accident in 1991. Sadiq had the contract on my head. Aftab Bhat had signed the dotted line. I killed Sadiq and disfigured his face. I gave up my identity, life, love, and my family to protect this nation against the leeches like Bhat.

I know there is no one apart from you who will believe a man hiding in a cave. None of my friends was in the car that went down the gorge. I dropped them at a shop on the highway and went ahead.

I was tired of living a dual life, of Aftab Bhat, his secrets and the entire system. I gave up. I am so sorry for not being there when your mother raised you. However, if I hadn't taken that step, you wouldn't be here. All of you would have been dead. A bullet in the head, like me. I know you will come, and when you do, I am sure you would want to murder me. I will make it easier for you.

Five feet below where I lay, are pictures and documents you might need to incinerate everyone involved in the turmoil of Kashmir. It might also prove my identity. Come back, collate everything here with the stuff you found at Bhat's residence and leak whatever is necessary.

Don't ever ask me, or God, the reason for what I am doing today. If not you, the security forces would put a bullet through me. I apologise for using you to destroy everyone. Aftab, his team, and all the recent attacks and blasts are on my head. Jahangir and others were, unfortunately, collateral damage.

For 30 years, I have worked with the deep state of both countries without revealing myself. I have chosen targets and executed plans in Kashmir to minimise the collateral damage. I have reported infiltration and killed scores of foreign mercenaries, but I have not been able to control the unrest and the outcome of the same. If I had killed Aftab Bhat and his team, his masters would have brought a new group in his place.

Someday, Kashmir might see a new dawn, but for that, Aftab Bhat has to depart. He proclaims to be a follower of peace, but the reality is that he relishes the unrest and gains power from it. Money is just a secondary source of lust. The power he wields over the top chairs in the system has gone beyond control.

If he doesn't die, the blasts and terror strikes will continue, and I won't be able to stop them. There are people in higher positions who are in charge. I have worked for many of them, but I have never gone against my country. It's finally the right time for me to come clean.

I have no regrets.

I have lived on my own terms. I shall die on my own.

When you are done, burn this letter and remember your father as the man who worked for India without once turning back to look at his family.

Signing off,

Yoginder Sharma, Solan.

Epilogue

A year had passed since I returned from the journey of a lifetime.

I never spoke to my mother or anyone about what actually happened that evening, but it remained etched in my memory. I escaped the hideout in time. The next morning, the picture of one of Kashmir's most wanted terrorists, Sadiq Khan, was published in all national and local newspapers.

The army claimed they shot him dead and recovered arms and ammunition. After escaping the encounter site, I stayed in the temple premises for some time. When the cordon eased off, I went back to Bijbehara. On the way, near a riverbed, I sat for hours reading the letter and wailing alone.

My father had come back to life for a minute before leaving me to the mercy of this cruel world yet again. I tore that piece of paper and threw it away in the river. I got up, wiped my tears and smiled. My life had found a new purpose.

A few hours after that incident, Varun informed Captain Sharma about the hidden bunker and unearthed documents that were worth gold. Many politicians and high-headed chairholders were now behind bars. This included the person with the satellite phone. All the evidence that was recovered from the hideout was leaked carefully.

The inquiry set up to investigate the murder of Aftab Bhat was shut down. Instead, an inquiry commission was now investigating fake encounters ordered by Aftab Bhat. There were media reports about how Sadiq Khan used to tip off security agencies about foreign terrorists and their hideouts, thereby helping the security agencies neutralise the threats.

The complete details of the recovery were never made public, but Captain Sharma told us that many bank accounts, hawala transactions, and money trails were tracked, and the perpetrators booked. The phenomenon called Aftab Bhat was dismantled, and the system he had carefully built up was broken brick by brick.

Today, Kashmir is not peaceful, but each one of us is working towards it.

I had resigned from my corporate job and decided to help my mother with a small business in the hills. We settled in the pristine town of Mattan. Our house overlooked the majestic Himalayas on one side and the magnificent Sun Temple on the other. We were trying to collaborate with the locals and start homestays.

The tourist influx was expected to begin once the situation around the world improved. Whenever I was in doubt, I stood near the windowsill and looked out, trying to comprehend what my father would have done had he been in my place.

The official chief of the Indian Intelligence sat in New Delhi and was in charge. Zeba Ji was the unofficial mentor. They say Zeba Ji's connections reached the highest level in Raisina Hill. Varun was the head of press affairs for the Governor of the Union Territory of Jammu and Kashmir.

My mother was back to her roots and seemed content. I, on the other hand, was enjoying the glory of breathing in the fresh air every morning without having to think about the past, which came alive by the actions of a man who only wanted to be a famous author.

Acknowledgements

This book is a result of many moments and people in my life. Coffee with my oldest friend, an article online that blew my mind, a man whom I have never seen but always wanted to, and a rockstar in the form of a literary agent.

Writers live many lives through their stories. Through this one, I lived like the man I always wanted to be. It moved me, made me cry, and made me give up, but for a change I sustained. After all, I was penning down probably the most important, yet the least talked about, tale of many around us—the quest of a son to find the truth about his father.

Firstly, I want to express gratitude to my brilliant literary agent, Suhail Mathur of The Book Bakers.

He believed in the story when no one else did. His support and faith have had a major impact on the journey of this book.

Thanks to the entire team at Vitasta Publishers for being there throughout the process.

Maa, thanks for believing in me when it mattered the most.

Vibha, my better half, thanks for motivating me to pursue my passions. Without you, I would have quit writing many moons back.

Advika, I hope you read this one fine day. I'm sure your questions about the story would be interesting.

Ruchi, thanks for bringing books into my life.

Amit, thanks for not letting me fall into the abyss when I was at my lowest.

Thanks to my uncles and aunts for fostering the courage I needed to dream.

Wikki, thanks for the spark that lit the fire of creativity inside me.

My friends, readers, and everyone else, I hope this tale inspires you to carve a path to find the reason for your existence.